se return / renew by date shown.

LANDS END

Visit us at www.boldstrokesbooks.com

By the Author

Infiltration

Lands End

LANDS END

by
Jackie D

2016

LANDS END

ISBN 13: 978-1-62639-739-2

This Trade Paperback Original Is Published By
Bold Strokes Books, Inc.
P.O. Box 249
Valley Falls, NY 12185

First Edition: September 2016

CREDITS
EDITORS: VICTORIA VILLASENOR AND CINDY CRESAP
PRODUCTION DESIGN: SUSAN RAMUNDO
COVER DESIGN BY JEANINE HENNING

Acknowledgments

Once again, thank you to Bold Strokes Books for believing in the stories that bounce around in my head. It is an honor and a privilege to be part of such a strong and supportive group of people. Thank you, Vic Villasenor, for being such a fantastic editor, understanding what I am trying to say, and always filling in the blanks that elude me. Thank you, Cindy Cresap, for your editing abilities and for your patience with my redundant issues (I swear I'm working on them). Thank you, Mom, for blazing through the manuscript with your accurate and always loving insights and corrections. Thank you to my friends and family for inspiring the characters in this particular book and a great deal of the interactions that take place.

Dedication

For Alexis and Stacy.

Alexis, there is not a version of reality where I would not find you and choose you, in this lifetime, or the next. Stacy, neither years nor distance will ever tarnish our friendship. Thank you for being my "Chloe."

CHAPTER ONE

"This is Amy Kline." Amy answered her phone while opening the garage door, blowing on her coffee, and adjusting the heel of her shoe. Multitasking was something she prided herself on, not only because she felt it was something akin to a sport, but also because it was an attribute she found most other people truly lacked the ability to do well. She liked being able to set herself apart from the rest of the crowd, in whatever ways she could.

"Amy! This is Charlie Turner over at the Miners."

Charlie was in the unfortunate predicament of needing Amy's assistance on a nearly monthly basis. Being the general manager for the Miners, a professional football team, probably had its perks, but needing a public relations firm on retainer, a very large retainer, probably wasn't one of them.

"Charlie! I was expecting a call from you. Please grab Frank and meet me down at my office in thirty minutes." There was silence on the other end of her phone. Amy smiled to herself. Charlie never had much of a stomach for the situations his players seemed to get themselves into. It was an endearing quality. "It's okay, Charlie. I've already been informed of the little incident this morning, and let me remind you, it's why you keep me on your payroll. Just grab Frank and get down to the office."

"See you in a bit then, Amy. Thank you."

She pushed the unlock button to her metallic gray Audi A6 and got in the driver's seat. This sleek, sexy machine was definitely not something she would have paid for herself. She hadn't read every page of the owner's manual, but she was almost convinced this car would fly if she could figure out the correct numeric combination on the touch screen monitor. It had been a payment for services from a client a few months prior. A payment Amy still believed was absolutely excessive, but he had insisted, and the senior partners told her to accept.

She pushed the button on the dash, and the car purred with a low subtlety Amy was growing to truly love. The phone rang through the speakers, and Amy pushed the talk button as she pulled out of her parking garage.

"Good morning, Ms. Kline."

Amy shook her head. "Sarah, how many times do I have to remind you to call me Amy? I feel like I'm either on the verge of my fiftieth birthday, or I'm going to morph into my mother every time you say that."

"Right, sorry about that. Force of habit when we're working. Anyway, I was calling with the updates for Peter Reynolds." Sarah was the best administrative assistant Amy had ever worked with. In fact, she was tossing around the idea of giving her a new title, something more in line with being an information superhero of some sort.

"Okay, great, let's go through what you've been able to find out so far." She heard a few clicks of the keyboard on the other end of the line.

"Well, as you already know, Peter was picked up outside a nightclub early this morning. He was intoxicated, getting ready to drive his vehicle, and had three girls with him."

Amy sipped her coffee and continued to maneuver through traffic while thinking that this would be a much easier day than she had anticipated. Football players managed to get themselves into a variety of deplorable situations, but this definitely didn't top the "most heinous" list. "This isn't a major emergency. We can spin the drunk in public part. He *wasn't* driving, and the girls are a non-issue since the pictures at the scene didn't divulge any compromising positions." Sarah didn't answer, an indication Amy had learned meant she was uneasy. "What is it?"

Sarah said, "All three girls were under seventeen."

Amy shook her head. *So much for an easy fix.* "Fantastic. I'll be there in fifteen." She clicked off the phone and continued with the rest of her drive. How people continued to get themselves into these situations was beyond her. It was good for business, sure, but she hated having to deal with these really messy circumstances, where it was nearly impossible to determine who needed the actual protection.

It had been five years since Amy had graduated top of her class at Brown, with a degree in English. Much to her parents' disappointment, she decided not to go to graduate school and instead took a job with a top tier public relations firm, Morgan & Morgan. She'd risen to the top quickly, and the rumor mill started spilling tidbits regarding her possible promotion to partner. This was something that had never been achieved by anyone working at the firm for less than ten years, much less a woman. Of course, along with these rumors came assumptions of sleeping her way to the top and other vulgar sexual favors. It always baffled her that people ignored the fact she was the first one into the office, last to leave, and never took a vacation. Her work was her life and she was happy with her success. Having a family or a significant other was never on her radar, and it wasn't something she felt was missing from her life. Despite her mother's incessant nagging that she wanted grandchildren.

The parking garage at the office was virtually empty, which was no big surprise for a Saturday morning. Most people were out enjoying their weekend with friends or family, or indulging in the endless variety of activities that San Francisco offered.

Amy loved the location of her office building. As she rode the elevator to the twenty-ninth floor, she looked out over the beautiful San Francisco Bay. It was a rare morning without the ever-present fog, and she could see the Bay Bridge. The early morning colors of red and orange coming off the water in shimmers gave her a moment of relaxation before her soon to be chaotic day pushed its way into her mind. The ding of the elevator signaled the end of solitude, and she turned around to find Sarah waiting as the doors slid open.

"Charlie and Frank actually beat you here. They're waiting in the conference room." Sarah took the empty travel mug from Amy's hand and replaced it with another cup of coffee, then took her briefcase and replaced it with her tablet.

Amy pushed the heavy glass door of the conference room open, and the two men stood up. "Good morning, gentlemen." The two nodded as they took their seats. Charlie pulled at his tie, a habit Amy had been trying to break him of, especially when he made television appearances. It wasn't often she needed to deal with both the general manager and the head coach, but in this situation, she wasn't surprised Frank had decided to come along. Having your star receiver in any type of trouble was never a good thing, but Amy assumed Frank was sweating even more because of the timing. She flipped through the images a passerby at this morning's scene had taken with his phone. He'd been in the process of trying to sell them to newspapers, but Sarah had been able to stall the process. But five hundred dollars only bought twenty-four hours these days. Enough time to figure out the best approach for damage control or worst-case scenario to try to buy the pictures back and silence the involved parties.

"These girls are young." Amy glanced at them and noted their pinched expressions. "The drunk in public predicament is an easy fix, except you have a game tomorrow and it could cause a distraction to Peter and the rest of the team." The men continued to stare, seemingly anxious to hear the rest of her analysis. "The age of these girls is an entirely different issue. We need to find out how serious this is. We need to determine if this is a habit or an anomaly. So we need to find out who these girls are."

Charlie rocked back in his chair and stared at the ceiling. "This job becomes more like being a babysitter every year."

Frank leaned across the table, the circles under his eyes and the gray in his hair that wasn't there two years ago, proof this job as head coach was taking its toll. "We have to fix this. We're two weeks from the playoffs, and we can't go into the post season without our number one wide receiver."

Amy sighed inwardly, ignoring the slight knot in her stomach. She wouldn't show the disgust she really felt. She was too professional for that. Her ability to compartmentalize was one of the things that set her apart from her peers. "Let me see what I can find out." Both men looked relieved. "Keep him at the training facility or at home. No going out, no social media, nothing until I can get this situation under control. Please advise his wife to follow the same restrictions. The last thing we need is for her to fly off the handle and exponentially increase the possibility of early media coverage."

Both men stood to leave, shook Amy's hand, and left for their respective missions. Amy followed, passing Wonder Assistant's desk. *No, too cliché.* Sarah followed Amy into her office and shut the door behind her.

Amy pinched the bridge of her nose and started thinking. "We have a lot of work to do and we only have twenty-four hours to do it."

❖

Lena's anger had reached a level she had yet to experience in her twenty-seven years. Her heart was palpitating, her vision seemed slightly blurred, and her hands were tingling. She was pacing up and down her living room. Her younger sister was sitting on the couch, arms folded, watching her unravel. "What the hell were you thinking?" It wasn't a rhetorical question. Lena really wanted to know the answer, but it wasn't coming fast enough. "You told me you were spending the night at Marcy's house, and then I get a phone call at five in the morning from the police department saying you were not only at a nightclub, but with a guy twelve years older than you, AND you were ready to get in his car, drunk!"

Her sister shook her head and looked away. "You don't even want to hear my side of the story!"

Lena stopped pacing and put her hands on her hips. "That's where you're wrong, Laura. Out with it."

Laura looked as if she was going to start crying, and her obvious distress pulled at Lena, but she forced herself to not give in.

"I don't know why you're so mad anyway. You did way worse when you were my age."

Damn it. "How would you know? You were only five years old when I was your age! What were you doing at that nightclub with that guy?"

Laura turned her head, shooting daggers at her with her glare. "*That guy* happens to be the number one wide receiver for the San Francisco Miners, and someone I'm casually dating."

Lena needed a mirror just to make sure there wasn't actually smoke coming out of her ears like a cartoon character. "Laura! You're sixteen years old! Every single one of your relationships needs to be casual, unless that *guy* is in his late twenties, in which case, it's illegal!"

"I'm not a child!" Laura stood up, mimicking Lena's stance.

Lena's voice was raised. She hated yelling at her sister, but this teenage specimen was a far cry from the sweet little sister she had once known. "You're most definitely still a child, and you're not going to keep seeing this guy."

Laura ran up the stairs. "Try and stop me!"

Before she heard the door slam shut, Lena yelled back, "You're grounded, by the way." The house shook with the force of the door being heaved with all her sister's might. Lena flopped onto the couch and put her head in her hands. "God, Mom, I don't know what I'm doing here. I miss you so much. I think sometimes I do far more damage than good." There was no response. There never was. Just the simple act of talking out loud to the silence made her feel better at moments like this. Being her little sister's guardian was never something she had planned on, or could have anticipated. But this was her reality, the only existence she had known for years. The pain had subsided some as the days, then years, ticked off the calendar, but it was always there, twinging right beneath the surface.

Lena shook off the memory. She was far from perfect, but she had made a promise that night, and was hell-bent on keeping it. She would keep Laura safe, no matter the cost or the circumstances, and she wasn't going to start making exceptions now. She grabbed her phone and walked out to her back patio.

A sleepy voice answered her call. "Why are you calling me at eight on a Saturday morning?"

Lena smiled. Her best friend Chloe tried to sound agitated, but Lena knew she wasn't. "Is there a specific law against keeping a minor locked in her room until she's of legal age?" She could hear Chloe adjusting her sitting position on the other end of the phone.

"I think I might be able to plead a case of self-defense or temporary insanity."

Lena leaned back in her chair. "Perfect."

Chloe, who didn't need further explanation as to whom they were speaking about, continued. "What did your Mini-Me do this time?"

❖

Sarah tapped against the glass door that led into Amy's office. "I have the names and contact information of the three girls who were with Peter Reynolds."

Amy swiveled her chair back and forth, tapping a pen against the side of her face. "Just the phone call every parent wants to get the week before Christmas."

Sarah gave her a confused look. "This type of thing normally doesn't bother you."

Amy shook her head. "Sexual promiscuity can't bother you in this business. It's the age of the girls that's gotten under my skin."

Sarah walked over and placed the folder on Amy's desk. "It's a thin line you straddle. I don't envy your position."

Amy cocked her head. "And here I thought you had aspirations to take my job one day."

Sarah let out a loud dramatic laugh. "No, thank you. I'm perfectly happy doing what I do. It pays the bills very nicely, and I never have to take my work home."

Amy smiled at her. "Thank you." Sarah nodded and closed the door behind her.

The first two phone calls went relatively well. The parents were willing to settle for a hefty sum of money in order to not press charges, with the understanding Peter Reynolds would go nowhere near their daughters again. They, in turn, would have to sign a confidentiality agreement. From the information she was able to gather through the phone conversations, Reynolds hadn't taken his relationship with these girls to a physical level. It seemed to be strictly to bolster his ego. Although she couldn't quite wrap her head around why a grown, married man, would need teenagers for that. Amy was about to make her last phone call when her phone beeped in, and Sarah's voice came through the speaker. "There's a Lena Michaels here to see you, the sister of Laura Michaels."

Amy closed her eyes. She knew this wasn't going to be an easy encounter. She didn't like being unprepared, and that was exactly what this Lena woman was doing, putting her in a situation where she didn't have an immediate upper hand. "Please show her into the conference room. I'll be in there in a moment."

Amy walked over to the small closet and pulled the door open to study herself in the full-length mirror. *Authority is ascertained in the first two minutes of every conversation.* She often repeated this phrase to herself before walking into an intense situation. She had learned very quickly in the all-boys club that was her work life, the upper hand was the only position you ever wanted to have, and first impressions often made the difference in the power differential. Amy checked for wrinkles in her black pinstriped suit, running her hands down each of her arms, then checked the clip that held back her coffee-colored hair. She was naturally a blonde but had dyed her hair prior to interviewing at Morgan & Morgan, in an attempt to be taken more seriously. She had read an article stating blonde women in the workplace were often placed into a male "fantasy file," regardless of how hard they worked or how good they were at their jobs. She brushed the hair away from her eyes, glad there weren't dark circles under them, and gave herself a reassuring smile. She closed the door, grabbed her tablet, and went down the hall to the conference room.

Amy took a moment to inspect the woman waiting in the excessively large conference room before she went in. She leaned against the window and looked like her thoughts were a million miles away. She was tall, taller than Amy's five-foot-four frame, and had the build of a runner, under her perfectly fitted jeans and plum sweater. Her dark chocolate hair was shoulder length and loose, and when she tucked it behind her ear, Amy was taken aback by her presence and the confidence she exuded. She shook it off and pushed into the room. "I'm

Amy Kline." There was a pause as Amy waited for the woman to face her, but she didn't, so Amy continued. "I understand you wanted to meet with me."

The woman continued to look out the window as Amy walked over and stood next to her. "No, I don't want to meet with you, Ms. Kline. I wanted to meet with Peter Reynolds. They told me that wasn't possible, so instead I'm forced to meet with you."

Amy remained silent, still waiting for this woman to have the decency to face her.

"My sister, Laura, is only sixteen years old." There was pain and worry in her voice.

"If you would like to take a seat, I'm sure we can work something out to your satisfaction, Ms. Michaels."

Lena turned and stared at Amy. Her stunning blue eyes were fierce, bold, and a little hardened. Lena was beautiful.

"My satisfaction? I seriously doubt that." Lena pulled out one of the impressive, large black leather chairs, and sat down.

She crossed her legs, and Amy felt her gaze as she took her seat and started flipping through the images on her tablet to distract herself for a moment. No one threw Amy off her game, but this woman's stare was doing just that. The heat coming off her body was unmistakable. There was fury behind her posture, her glower, her presence. Amy wondered if her passion was as high in other areas. "What can I do to help you, Ms. Michaels?" Amy looked Lena in the eyes, her unbridled confidence pushing to the surface, intending to push back against the woman in front of her.

Lena shook her head and looked back down at the table, crossing her arms. "How can you cover up for people like this? How do you even sleep at night?"

The insult cut in a way that didn't usually bother her. "You're insinuating that I have some knowledge about this situation. All I know is Peter Reynolds was at a nightclub with

three underage girls. As far as I know, that's all that happened."
Amy willed her mouth to stay shut, but her defenses were on
high alert. "I guess my question is, why was a minor in your
care out with him in the first place?" Amy wished she could take
it back as soon as the words left her mouth. A scowl washed
over the woman's face, and she knew she had wounded her.
"Look, Ms. Michaels—"

"You can call me Lena." She was still looking at the table,
but her voice had softened. She looked defeated, in a way.

"Lena." Amy wanted to reach for her hand, but she stopped
herself. "Did something else happen that you need to tell me
about?"

The anger reignited, sizzling white-hot at the surface. The
heat again started to radiate off her body. "Why? So you can
get the correct information to cover up?" Lena didn't give her
a chance to respond. "I want him to stay away from Laura. No
contact whatsoever. If you can't make this happen, I'll file for
a restraining order. The only thing stopping me from going to
the police right now is the media circus that would immediately
surround my sister, but I will if you force my hand."

Lena stood to leave when Amy interrupted. "The team
is willing to make restitution if you'll sign a confidentiality
agreement. Currently, there are no lawyers involved, as we
don't see the need, so the process can be streamlined." Amy felt
dirty even saying it. She shouldn't. This was her job, it's what
she was good at, but for some reason she didn't want Lena to
have ill feelings about her.

Lena stopped and turned around. "The team wants to pay
me to keep my mouth shut?"

"It would be unfortunate if you saw it that way. They
merely want to compensate you for any trouble or heartache
this occurrence has caused."

Lena shook her head and continued toward the door. "Just
keep him away from my sister and we shouldn't have any more

problems. According to her, they're dating. Make sure that isn't true." The door didn't slam shut, it wasn't built to, but it was the loudest sound Amy had ever heard.

Sarah quickly came into the room. "Everything okay?"

Amy was still trying to put into perspective what exactly had just taken place. "I'm not sure okay is the right word for what just happened."

Sarah frowned and shifted her weight. "While you were in your meeting, I did some digging on Lena and Laura Michaels."

Amy raised her eyebrows, waiting for Sarah to continue.

"They're the daughters of Bradley and Michelle Michaels."

Amy didn't give any indication she knew who Sarah was talking about, and Sarah rolled her eyes.

"I swear the only people you know in this city are the ones that need their images spit-shined. They owned Lands End, the beautiful restaurant out on the point. They were killed about seven years ago in a robbery gone bad, very bad. Lena was in college at the time at UC Davis, and Laura was only nine. Laura was in the restaurant when it happened. Lena moved home to become Laura's guardian and took over Lands End."

Amy leaned back again in her chair and looked out the window at the city below. She could barely make out the sparkling Pacific Ocean, as the buildings obstructed her view from this particular room, a fact she always found frustrating. Looking at the water cleared her mind, quieted her chaos, and brought warmth to her chest. She was trying to find her peace, her serenity, because suddenly protecting her client wasn't at the forefront of her mind. Protecting this stranger was something she seemed to feel instinctually, and it was unsettling. Sarah's voice pulled her from her internal reflection.

"Thoughts?"

Amy let her weight shift the chair back to its normal position. "Well, we'll have to handle this a bit more delicately. This family has a presence in the city, and the last thing we need is for a very sweet, young, orphaned Laura Michaels to end up on the front page with Peter Reynolds." She felt goose bumps crawl along her unexposed arms all the way up to her neck. The ability to say the previous sentence out loud was what made her good at her job, but it didn't make it any easier. *How many underage girls would there be? How many cheating spouses? How many cover-ups?*

Chapter Two

L ands End could have been the setting in a romantic comedy, according to Chloe, who stated exactly that on a monthly basis. It was nestled on the farthest point of the San Francisco peninsula. Every seat in the restaurant had a perfect view of the Bay Bridge, the Golden Gate Bridge, and Alcatraz. This particular evening, the fog had wrapped itself around the exterior like a blanket. The warm lights coming from the inside brought a feeling of home, of family. Lena rolled down the window of her car, despite the cool night air, in order to hear the waves smashing into the rocks of the cove. She always felt closest to her parents here. At times, Lena could almost hear her mother's laughter coming from the main dining area. For a moment, Lena let herself believe she was really there, about to come around the corner.

Lena was so caught up in her thoughts she didn't hear Chloe calling her name until she was right beside the window.

"Hey there!"

Lena gasped, startled out of her reverie.

"Whoa! I didn't mean to scare you. I was calling your name. I figured you heard me."

Lena shook her head, rolled up the window, and got out of the car. "Sorry, I got a little lost there for a second."

Chloe put her arm around Lena's shoulders. "You okay, Lee?"

Lena smiled. The nickname had been hers since grade school, and although she wasn't necessarily fond of it, she loved that it was something special between her and Chloe. "Yeah, I'm fine. Just a little preoccupied."

Chloe bumped her side. "Well, I don't know why. You have absolutely no reason to be. You run one of the most successful restaurants in the Bay Area, you're raising a teenager that has a thing for professional football players, and you haven't had sex in two years. You should really stop complaining and bask in the ease that is your everyday life."

Chloe kissed her on the cheek, and Lena gasped playfully. "It has not been two years, for your information. It has only been eighteen months." She paused briefly. "Give or take."

Chloe got a few steps ahead turned around to walk backward. "That's my point, Lee! If you don't know the last time, it's been way too long!"

She opened the door and Lena walked past her. "Let's not talk about my sex life here."

Chloe took off her jacket as they walked inside. "I'm a customer and I will talk about whatever I please."

Lena rolled her eyes. "You haven't paid for a meal here in your entire life."

"That's not the point." Chloe sat at her favorite table in the corner.

"I have a few things to check on, and then I'll come eat with you."

Chloe flipped through the wine menu. "Don't bother. I'm meeting a friend."

Lena put her hands on her hips. "A friend huh? What's his name?"

"*Her name* is Evelyn and she is a transfer from our New York office. I'm being friendly."

"Friendly, or scoping the competition for single men?"

"Friendly. She bats for your team."

Lena leaned down, so her voice wouldn't carry across the restaurant. "Please don't set me up. Whatever you're doing, please don't. Not right now."

Chloe leaned back. "Easy, tiger. I meant it when I said I'm just being friendly. Not everything revolves around you." She gave Lena a playful wink.

Lena sighed and walked toward the kitchen. She didn't want to risk being there when Chloe's friend arrived.

Amy opened a bottle of her favorite white wine, walked out onto her patio, and stretched out on one of her lounge chairs. The patio was the reason she had picked this apartment. Well, the patio, the closet, and the parking garage. Finding just one of these amenities in a San Francisco apartment was like striking gold. Finding all three was nothing short of a supernatural phenomenon. She sipped her wine and thought back to the woman she had met earlier that day. *Lena Michaels.* There was something about her that tugged at Amy. She swirled the wine in her glass and sipped it absently. Her phone rang, and she glanced down at the caller ID and smiled. "I thought you said you liked your job because you didn't have to take your work home with you."

"I'm not taking my work home with me. I actually wanted to see if you felt like having a drink. You looked like you needed one when you left the office today."

"I actually already beat you to it. I'm having a glass of wine now. You're welcome to join me."

"Perfect, I'm just around the corner. I'll be there in a minute."

Amy walked toward her front door. When the buzzer rang, she pushed the button and then pulled out another glass.

Sarah came around the corner and into the kitchen. Amy watched her as she looked around the space. Sarah always seemed to be taking in details and a mental inventory of her surroundings. She'd been to Amy's apartment several times, occasionally to work, and other times for nights like this.

Candles burned throughout the area, infusing the air with wonderful holiday aromas. Amy loved the serenity candles gave off, and she made a point to light them whenever she wanted to relax. Every cabinet and countertop was pure, polished white, with chrome finishing. It was a perfect contrast to the dark hardwood floors and wooden bar top. The track lighting matched the chrome fixtures perfectly, and when dimmed, brought a sense of warmth to what should have been a cold, modern space. Sarah placed the bottle of wine on the bar.

Amy grabbed it and smiled. "Good, one bottle for you and one for me."

Sarah sat on the bar stool and shook her head with a smile. "This isn't my first time here."

Amy poured the wine and motioned to the living room. She flipped a switch on the wall, and the fireplace flickered on from the other side of the room. They sat on opposite ends of the couch, quiet for a moment, enjoying the warmth.

"Is Matt going home with you for Christmas?"

Sarah nodded. "He is. He should be back from Los Angeles tomorrow evening. We'll be headed to my parents' house in Marin on Christmas Eve morning."

"What's he doing in Los Angeles?"

Sarah sipped her wine, looking as though she was concentrating. "He went down there for training. He was promoted to detective, and they have a large training facility down there. He was taking a three-week course in investigation hosted by the FBI."

Amy shifted, putting her legs and feet under her. "Have you given him an answer yet? About the proposal?"

Sarah grinned wryly. "Maybe this whole becoming friends thing wasn't a great idea. It seems I've spilled my guts to you on more than one occasion while drinking."

Amy laughed. "I think we do fantastically, separating our lives into personal and professional, and you, my *friend,* are evading the question."

"I love him, I really do. I've never loved someone or something more, in fact. I just…I guess…ugh! Look at me stumbling over my words, so much for being Assistant Extraordinaire."

Amy shook her head. "Your assistant skills aren't in question, not now, and not since you walked into my office. I do like the name though. Maybe I can get you a cape of some kind."

Sarah inclined her head to acknowledge the compliment. She continued. "I don't want to end up a statistic, getting married at twenty-three, pregnant at twenty-four, and divorced at twenty-six." Sarah sipped again as soon as the statement left her mouth, like the words were some type of filth she couldn't wait to wash away.

"I don't know if you want my opinion or not, especially since I have absolutely no foundation to give any type of love advice." She paused to give Sarah another comforting smile. "But if it's right, it's right. It doesn't matter if you're twenty-two, twenty-nine, or fifty-five."

Sarah seemed to be mulling over what Amy had said as she stared at the fire.

"What about you?" Sarah asked, snapping out of her trance.

"Ha! What about me?"

"Well, you're a beautiful, successful, creative woman. Why isn't there a ring on your finger?"

Amy shook her head and glanced down at her left hand. "I've never really made time for it, I guess." She had never talked about Evie to anyone except Addison, especially anyone in her life in San Francisco. She had never even told Sarah she was attracted to women and not men.

"Well, not making time for it, and not wanting it, are two separate things, aren't they?"

Amy nodded. "I guess they are." Amy shifted in her seat, uncomfortable discussing her love life other than as a joke.

"If you're trying to figure out whether or not to tell me you're gay, I already know."

Amy sighed. "That shouldn't surprise me. I've never met anyone better at obtaining information."

"It was nothing I obtained, just something I figured out."

Amy looked up, from one side to the other with an intentional, overdramatic flare. "I thought for sure I had the glowing sign that hung over my head removed."

Sarah laughed. "Hardly! I can just tell. I'm naturally observant. When we had lunch a few weeks ago and I asked who your last serious relationship was, you used non-descriptive pronouns about someone in college. All the pictures in your office, and in your home, are with other women, or your family. Plus, every company function we've ever had, you always come alone. Even single employees usually bring a date to enjoy the free booze and food."

Amy finished the last of her wine in a big gulp. "Impressive. And here I thought I had to keep my Birkenstock collection hidden with you around."

Sarah almost spit wine through her nose. "I seriously doubt you, Amy Kline, have ever let a pair of those near your feet."

Amy laughed. "That would be a correct assumption. I don't even know where to purchase them."

"Well, since we're in San Francisco, I'd assume Haight-Ashbury."

Amy laughed. She loved Sarah's sense of humor, and it was nice to be around someone she didn't have to pretend with.

"I should really get going." Sarah got up to leave. "I didn't realize how late it was getting, and I'm meeting a friend of mine for breakfast and shopping in the morning."

Amy got up and walked her to the door. "Thanks for stopping by." Amy gave her a hug and realized it was the first time in a long while she'd touched another person. The thought made her sad, but she hid it. *No sense in letting her see the cracks.* "See you Monday morning."

"Yes, ma'am!" Sarah gave her a salute before disappearing into the elevator.

Lena watched cautiously from the safety of the kitchen, waiting for Chloe's dinner companion to come through the door. The clanging of the pots and pans, combined with the chatter of the kitchen staff, offered a supportive, soothing hum of background noise. Her mother had been an amazing chef, and even if Lands End had been placed at the top of a ridge people would have to climb a mountain to reach, there would still be a line outside the door. That exact statement was given by a very popular Bay Area food critic about a year before Michelle Michaels was killed. Lena, on the other hand, was lucky if she didn't burn toast. She always found it a little ludicrous that she managed to pick up absolutely nothing from the hours she spent in this kitchen as a child watching her mother's every move, and tasting every new recipe, giving the "Lena stamp of approval."

She walked back over to the table. Chloe was flipping through her phone and looking pouty. "What's up?" Lena casually asked.

"It seems I've been stood up. She's decided to put in a few more hours at the office."

Lena sat at the table, crossing her hands. "I don't think you understand what being stood up means."

Chloe sipped her wine. "I really wanted you to meet her."

Lena chuckled. "I knew you were trying to set me up!"

Chloe shook her head and tried to look innocent. "No! I was simply trying to expand your friend base. I know I'm absolutely amazing, but there simply isn't enough of me to go around."

Lena smiled. "There is if you account for the size of your ego. We could always divide that up and there would be enough Chloe for the entire world."

Chloe stuck her tongue out at Lena. "You're funny. It's good you remind me of that from time to time."

Lena stood up and pushed her chair under the table. "Let me go grab us some dinner."

Amy was back on her balcony, watching the city lights and listening to the noises that made San Francisco feel like a friend, and not just a city. With a blanket draped over her, and a glass of wine in her hand, she felt toasty and secure. Her thoughts slipped back to the day's events. She was a little frustrated with herself, not being able to pinpoint why she was unable to get Lena Michaels out of her head. It wasn't just the way she looked, although that didn't hurt. Her loose hair, perfectly defined jawbone, and lean, muscular body certainty stimulated Amy's libido, but it was more than that. Lena was fiercely protective of her younger sister, the way a mother would be. Amy guessed there was nothing Lena wouldn't do for the teenager, no length she wouldn't go to. Her love was apparent and deep. She not only respected that about Lena, she wanted that type of endless, fervent love in her life as well. The frightening part was, she never realized it was something she would consider wanting again. She grabbed the phone to call Addison and then thought better of it. It was late in New York, and she didn't want to wake up her sister.

She glanced down at her watch. Nine thirty. *Will Lena still be at the restaurant?* She felt a bit like a stalker, as she considered going down to the famed restaurant, to try to get a glimpse into the woman she couldn't get out of her mind. *There's nothing wrong with wanting to take in local culture.* She shook her head. *I can't believe I'm trying to justify this to myself.* Regardless, she got out of her chair and went into her closet to change clothes. Amy opted for a pair of jeans, a green V-neck sweater, and a pair of plain black boots. She looked herself up and down in the mirror. *Casual, but still interesting.* She grabbed her coat and headed down to the street before she had time to talk herself out of it.

CHAPTER THREE

Lena and Chloe fell into their easy conversation as each ate a salad and shared the cheese bread that Chloe swore she would give up sex for, if the absurd ultimatum were ever to be given.

There was a break in the conversation, and Chloe said, "Penny for your thoughts?"

Lena shook her head. "A penny, huh?"

Chloe shrugged. "Okay, with inflation, how about a dollar?"

Lena smiled. Chloe always had that effect on her. No matter how bizarre her day was, Chloe was a happy space. "Just thinking about earlier today." Lena knew her face often gave away her emotions. She typically tried to hide it, but it wouldn't have mattered with Chloe anyway. Lena knew Chloe could see right through her.

"The PR rep you met with?"

Lena nodded. She let out a small huff to accentuate her annoyance.

"What was her name again? Maybe I can dig something up on her and make her life a little more difficult."

Lena glanced at the door and almost choked on a piece of bread. "Amy Kline."

"Do you know if that's with a C or a K?"

Lena shook her head and pointed toward the door with her fork. "No. Amy Kline." She was standing at the front door, looking somewhat shell-shocked, returning Lena's gaze.

"Oh, wow," Chloe muttered. "That explains why she has you all out of sorts."

Amy was walking over, but Lena managed to shoot Chloe a dirty look before Amy was close enough to see it.

There was nothing Lena could do to escape. Amy's stride was purposeful and seemed intent, but her expression looked a bit unsure. By the time she made it to the table, she seemed even more unsettled. Lena stood when Amy was within a foot. "Can I help you with something?"

Amy appeared to be at a loss for words, which was probably out of character, if Lena had to guess. A slight blush crossed her face and she looked away. "I was in the area, having dinner with a friend, and thought I would stop in for a drink."

Lena was torn. She wasn't sure she wanted to be near this woman, but for some reason, she didn't want her to leave either.

Amy looked at Chloe, and a look of panic crossed her face. "I'm so sorry. I didn't mean to intrude."

Chloe smiled. "Oh, you aren't intruding on anything."

Lena knew Chloe was watching her, probably trying to gauge her reaction to the gorgeous woman in front of her. Lena tried to focus on seeming unfazed. "Is there something I can help you with?" She was irritated, and her voice mimicked her feelings, but she couldn't decide if she was irritated with Amy, Chloe, or herself.

Amy seemed worried by Lena's reaction. "I didn't mean to upset you, Lena. I wanted to apologize if I came off as brash earlier. I can't begin to imagine—"

Lena cut her off before she could continue. "Did you come to snoop around? See if there was another way the Miners could exploit my sister?" Lena hated herself for the way her voice bristled with anger and accusation, but she wouldn't show it. She crossed her arms to prove a point she wasn't sure she wanted to make.

Amy pushed her hair out of her eyes, and Lena couldn't tell if she was thinking of a response or trying to keep her emotions in check, but her perfect green eyes seemed to shimmer with regret. "Again, I'm sorry for upsetting you. I should get going." Amy turned to leave.

Lena's stomach clenched. She wanted to stop her and apologize, ask her to stay, but she didn't move. Amy walked out without saying another word or looking back. Lena sat back down at the table and looked at Chloe, who was giving her a sideways stare.

"Was that necessary?"

Lena ran her hands over her face and tucked her hair behind her ears. "Not even eight hours ago, that woman tried to pay me off to protect some football player that's going after Laura."

"Isn't that her job?"

"Yeah, I guess. I think it's deplorable."

Chloe raised her eyebrows. "You know I'm a lawyer, right?"

"What does that have to do with anything?"

"I'm just glad that you don't judge me based on the people that I have to represent on a daily basis."

"That's different."

"Is it?"

"Yes, it is. You're…well…you." Chloe didn't respond. "This is Laura we're talking about, and I don't want anything to happen to her. Who knows what lengths this woman will go to, to protect that guy." Lena spun a fork in a quick circle on the clean, crisp tablecloth. "I mean, sure, she's beautiful. She's smart. She has this confidence about her that's kind of hot." She looked up at Chloe again. "But that doesn't mean I would be interested in her."

"Obviously."

Lena rolled her eyes at Chloe's predictable, sarcastic tone. "Don't do that."

"Don't do what?"

"Don't be all…I don't know…*you*." Lena got up and walked into the kitchen before Chloe could respond. She wasn't mad at Chloe; that wouldn't have been fair. She was irritated that Amy had such an effect on her. She was out of sorts and didn't like it. She wanted to be steadfast, decisive, and stubborn. Chloe was making it difficult to be all of those things without issue.

Lena pulled into the garage at their house on Diamond Street, near the Castro. Her parents had the forethought to buy the house in the early eighties, and it was paid off before Lena left for college. Lena truly loved the house, just as much for the location as for the airy rooms and the natural lighting. The kitchen, of course, was a chef's dream, but Lena felt the space was still her mother's. Her parents had been good with their money, and neither Lena nor Laura would ever have to worry about much, if they continued to handle it appropriately. Lena grabbed a bottle of water out of the glass refrigerator and sat on the couch. Over the years, Lena had replaced all of the furniture in the house, because there were too many memories tied up with each inanimate object. She looked at the only other item she had kept, a beautiful painting of the tree of life. The grays and blacks matched her furniture, as well as the sharp contrast to her own personal misfortunes. The painting should have made her sad, but it always managed to do the opposite. Rather, it kept her calm, and even hopeful at moments when it felt like the world was too much to deal with. The large windows afforded an amazing view of the city blocks below.

Laura came down the stairs silently. She stopped momentarily in front of the Christmas tree and moved an ornament that was drooping. Lena watched her, trying to figure out if she was feeling guilty or stalling.

"Can I have my phone back?"

Lena leaned her head back against the sofa. "Work was fine, thank you for asking."

Laura gave an irritated sigh. "How was work?"

"I just told you it was fine." This awarded her a small laugh from Laura, something that wasn't easy to come by. "Tell you what, you can have it back once I change your number and delete Peter Reynolds's."

Laura crossed her arms, and Lena knew she was already building a retort in her mind. "Before you say that isn't fair, let me be very clear…I don't care if it's fair. I don't care if you're mad, and I don't care if you think I'm the worst thing that has ever happened to you. I love you, and it's my job to protect you, even when you don't think you need protecting."

Laura was wiping tears away from her eyes, but Lena knew they were from anger and not from her heartfelt explanation.

"Is that it?"

Lena hated this part of their relationship. She should be giving her clothing and makeup advice, relationship advice, filling her in about the dos and don'ts of her impending college adventures. Anything but this. "No, that's not it. You're still grounded, and I need help at the restaurant next week."

"Perfect punishment, spending more time with you."

Lena had to keep herself from wincing. "Believe it or not, I don't like having to do this."

"Then don't!" Laura yelled.

"You didn't leave me a choice. Make childish decisions and I'll have no other choice than to treat you like a child."

Laura huffed. "Whatever!" She disappeared back up the stairs.

At least she didn't slam the door this time. Not a moment had passed before she heard the loud bang from her sister's bedroom door. "Never mind."

CHAPTER FOUR

Amy went for her run early in the morning, not only because her schedule demanded it, but because she loved this time of day. It was the time before the streets were inundated with commuters and hurried drivers. Smells from different bakeries and coffee shops saturated the thick, foggy, December air. She turned the corner and almost immediately turned around to take another route when she saw Lena sitting outside at a coffee table a few feet away. Lena glanced in her direction and their eyes met. Since it was too late to pretend she hadn't seen her, Amy walked over. Lena was dressed in running pants and a fleece top as well.

Amy couldn't think of anything to say. "Out running?" *Well, that was lame.*

Lena looked down at her clothes and then back up at Amy. "I know I'm no fashion icon, but I like to think I would dress a little more appropriately for work."

Amy couldn't do anything right when it came to Lena. She didn't need that kind of hassle. She went to put her ear buds back in when she felt Lena's hand on her arm.

"Amy, I'm kidding. Would you like to join me for coffee?"

Amy looked around, almost certain she was being Punk'd.

"Don't worry. I don't have anyone lying in wait to take you out, if that's what you're thinking."

"As a matter of fact," Lena continued as Amy sat down, "I wanted to apologize for the way I brushed you off the other night. I don't normally behave like that. I understand you have a job to do. Just please understand that I'll go to any length to protect the bratty, self-indulgent, little know-it-all I'm related to."

Lena's smile assured Amy that she was kidding again, and she felt at ease. Despite the fact she'd hardly done any running, she really wanted to stay. "I'm going to grab a cup of coffee and join you."

Lena nodded. "Please do. I don't have to be at work for several hours. I assume you've got a stricter schedule."

Amy got up to walk inside, glad Lena was willing to stick around. "I'm actually not working today."

A few minutes later, Amy came back outside with her steaming cup of coffee. She sat across from Lena, still a little dumbfounded how this situation was unfolding.

"So tell me, how is it you managed to get a day off with all of the scoundrels running loose on our streets? Has no one participated in anything epically stupid in the last few days?"

Amy laughed. "I'm sure someone has, but the managing partners have very strict rules about working this week. They want everyone to be with their families today, Christmas Eve, and Christmas. I figured I'd take advantage of it for once." Amy felt Lena's stare. She quickly tried to remember if she'd ever actually considered the way someone else saw her, outside of her professional environment. Lena's expression wasn't judgmental or pervasive, but rather it seemed appreciative, curious, and intense.

"Are you spending Christmas with your family?"

Amy was used to the question, but it made her a little more sad than usual. "I'm actually not this year. My sister Addison works for the *New York Times*, and she left this morning for some special assignment overseas that apparently can't wait until after the holidays." Amy gave a small chuckle. "My parents are on an 'Around the World in 180 Days' cruise. They'll be back in about a month."

Lena whistled. "That's impressive. I would love to do something like that."

Amy smiled at her. "My parents are amazing. I swear they seem to get younger the older they get. Does that make sense?"

Lena smiled back. "Perfect sense. Happiness will do that for you."

Amy thought briefly about asking Lena about her parents, but decided against it. Lena stood up and stretched. Amy had briefly appreciated Lena for a passing moment the morning they had met in her office, but the jeans hadn't done her any justice. The tight running pants that hugged her legs accentuated every muscle. As Lena's arms went above her head, the lower part of her stomach was exposed, and Amy briefly wondered what Lena's skin would feel like against her mouth. She snapped herself out of her reverie, fearing it would be noticed. She stood up and copied Lena's movements, needing to do something with her body. She was about to say good-bye when Lena turned to her.

"My house isn't far from here. Do you want to have breakfast with me?"

Amy was caught off guard, but couldn't think of anything she could possibly want more in that moment. "Yes, I'd like that."

The walk to Lena's house wasn't a long one. Amy had always enjoyed the architecture of San Francisco. The houses that lined the older sections of the city held stories and history unique to the city and the area. Amy wished the buildings could talk, so she could ask them questions about all they'd experienced. She didn't mention it to Lena, not wanting to sound like a crazy person.

When they walked through the front door of Lena's house, Amy loved it immediately. The space felt like a home, not just a house. She wanted to touch the walls, to hear the stories they could tell of the little girls that lived here with their parents. She smiled, thinking of a small Lena, filled with vigor and a sassy mouth she had apparently never lost.

Lena called to her from the kitchen, pulling her away from her thoughts. "I have a confession to make."

Amy looked at her sideways. Confessions in her line of work were never a good thing.

"I can't cook."

Amy laughed, relieved at the normality of the statement. "You own Lands End and can't cook?"

Lena laughed too. "I know it's ridiculous…but true." She shrugged apologetically.

Amy walked around the island and into the kitchen. "Let me see what I can do." She had no trouble finding everything she needed. The kitchen was set up very logically. It was obvious a chef had lived here.

Lena sat on the bar stool watching Amy. "I kept everything the same."

Amy didn't say anything. She just smiled, hoping Lena would continue. She liked the sound of her voice.

"After she died, I couldn't bear to change anything. I think I was worried that if I did, she'd really be gone forever."

The loss was etched on Lena's beautiful face, and Amy wanted to comfort her, but she was rooted to the spot. Comforting people wasn't her thing, and she had no idea where to begin.

Lena shook her head. "I'm so very sorry. I have no idea why I said that. I've never said that out loud to anyone."

Amy wanted to know more, but she thought changing the topic was probably the best idea. "Did you go to college?"

Lena seemed relieved at the shift in focus. "I went to UC Davis. I was going to get my degree in social work, and then hopefully my master's."

Amy switched between moving eggs around in a pan and cutting up a variety of fruit on the cutting board. "Did you ever think of going back?"

Lena walked over to the fridge and grabbed a pitcher of orange juice. Amy assumed it was fresh because of the plethora of orange peels she had seen in the trash can when she threw the eggshells away.

"Sure, I've thought about how it's not going to happen. That's not my life anymore."

Amy wanted to say more, wanted to tell her she should still be going after whatever she wanted, but a set of footsteps was rapidly pounding down the steps.

Laura frowned, looking back and forth between them. Lena spoke before the young woman Amy had recognized from the pictures had the chance. "Laura, this is Amy Kline. Amy, this is my younger sister, Laura."

"Don't you mean your prisoner?" Laura shot back.

Amy couldn't help but smile. Raising a teenager seemed to be about as trying as climbing Mt. Everest, and probably just as nerve-wracking. Laura poured herself a bowl of cereal and sat at the table. Their conversation halted, and Amy struggled with the uncomfortable silence.

Lena looked at her sister. "I need your help at the restaurant tonight."

Laura briefly stopped chewing, seemingly about to make some retort, but just nodded instead. "Can I go to Marcy's?"

"Are you still grounded?"

"Yes, but I don't see why."

"I'm not having this conversation with you right now."

Laura looked over at Amy, who was trying to focus on eating the eggs she had just placed on their plates without looking at the sisters.

"What if I check in every hour?"

Lena seemed to think about it for a moment. "I want you to check in every hour by calling me…from their land line."

Laura seemed to find this a satisfactory agreement. She grinned, rinsed her bowl, and ran back upstairs. The tension just as quickly drained from the room, and Lena sighed.

Amy smiled. "She's very pretty and very…what's the word…"

Lena chuckled. "I think the term you're looking for is pain in the ass."

Amy laughed. "No, she's just a teenager."

A brief look of pain and anger crossed Lena's face. "This—us becoming friends"—she pointed her fork between herself and Amy—"doesn't change the fact that I don't want that man anywhere near her."

Amy was a bit hurt Lena would think she'd do something so tawdry, but she took a deep breath and reminded herself that Lena was just protecting her little sister. *Addison would have done the same.* "Is that what we are now? Friends?"

Lena stared at her with so much focus and intent, had she been standing, her knees would have buckled. Lena was intense, passionate, and her gaze was unlike anything Amy had experienced.

"I would like that."

Amy felt her face flush. "I'd like that too." Amy fought every part of her mind that told her not to touch, not to desire. But, Lena's chiseled features called to a place Amy hadn't explored in a very long time. Lena seemed to feel the same draw as she touched the top of Amy's hand. Amy wanted the touch to continue, to go further. Lena's stare was intent on Amy's mouth as she moved her hand up her arm and then to her neck. Amy let out a breath filled with longing and desire. Lena started to pull Amy closer, her eyes closed, welcoming the kiss, her lips parted. They looked so soft, so inviting.

The front door slammed.

"Lena!" someone yelled. "I know it's early! I didn't have my phone or I would have—" The statement cut off as Chloe walked into the kitchen. Lena still had her hand on top of Amy's, but she quickly removed it when she saw Chloe glance down. Chloe dropped her purse on the counter. She crossed her arms and gave an inquisitive stare. "Am I interrupting?"

Lena walked over to the counter to pour coffee. "What's up, Chloe?"

Chloe kept her eyes on Amy for a moment before turning her attention to Lena. "I was seeing if you wanted to have breakfast, because you typically forget to do things like that on the twenty-third of every month."

"I actually just ate."

Chloe eyed the dishes sitting around the kitchen. "I see that. I also know you can barely create an edible Pop-Tart, so I'm going to assume you did the cooking?" She looked at Amy.

"Nice to see you again, Chloe."

Chloe smiled at her, and Amy could tell she was trying to put the pieces together. *Does Chloe think I stayed the night?* For some reason, she didn't want Lena's friend thinking there was something shady going on. "I didn't…we didn't…we ran into each other this morning at the coffee shop." Amy knew she was blushing, probably making herself much less believable.

Lena seemed to sense she was uncomfortable. "Knock it off, Chloe. We ran into each other at the coffee shop and Amy made us eggs. Very good eggs, I might add."

Chloe feigned offense, holding her hand against her chest. "I didn't say anything."

Laura had come back down the stairs and was watching the exchange. She rolled her eyes, kissed Chloe on the cheek, and waved to Lena.

"Be at Lands End by five." The door shut a moment later.

Amy got up from the table and placed her plate in the sink. "I should get going." She gave Lena a small, private smile. "Thank you for this morning."

Lena followed her to the front door. Amy was sure she'd never felt someone's presence so acutely.

"Thank you for breakfast."

Amy cocked her head to the side. "Thank you for inviting me. I really did enjoy it."

Lena looked like she wanted to say more. She chewed on her bottom lip, seemingly considering something, and the unconscious action was very sexy. Amy briefly wanted to know more, to know everything. Lena was intriguing and beautiful. Amy was accustomed to beautiful, but she wasn't used to this kindness that seemed to pulse out of Lena. There was so much warmth about her. Lena looked back toward the kitchen and seemed to change her mind about whatever it was she was going to ask. She reached around Amy's body, and for that split second, Amy wasn't sure if her heart had stopped, or was going to burst from her chest. But Lena simply pulled the door open, much to Amy's disappointment. The cool morning air that crashed against her back was exactly what she needed. She stood on her tiptoes and kissed Lena on the cheek. The side of Lena's face was warm and soft. Once again, Amy felt a tingling sensation that shot from her feet to her fingertips. Lena leaned closer. Her mouth was at her ear, and Amy could feel her breath.

"I hope we run into each other again."

Amy wanted to say something. Talking, persuasion, banter. That's where Amy excelled; that was what she was paid to succeed at.

She pulled her face away from Lena. "You know where to find me." She walked out the door without looking back, without saying anything else. Words eluded her, perhaps for the first time in her life. *What is wrong with me?*

CHAPTER FIVE

Lena shut the door and turned around to go back into the kitchen. Amy's scent was still permeating her senses. She ran straight into Chloe, who was coming out of the kitchen.

"Jesus, Chloe." She moved past her, but Chloe wasn't going to go away until she got the answers she wanted. Lena knew that for a fact.

"What was that?

Lena sipped her coffee. "What was what?"

Chloe put one hand on her hip and tapped the counter. "Oh, is that what we're going to do? You're going to make me ask you the same question one hundred different ways, when we both know what the outcome is going to be. You're going to tell me. You can't even help it; we're both prewired to tell the other."

Lena nodded, knowing it was true. "It was breakfast, Chloe. That's all."

Chloe looked at her skeptically. "That was not just breakfast, Lena Michaels. You two looked like you were going to devour each other."

Lena shook her head. "I don't know what you're talking about."

Chloe let out a long, dramatic sigh and grabbed her purse to leave. "I'll play your little game for now. But I'll be watching."

Lena smiled. "See you tonight?"

Chloe glanced over her shoulder before she left. "Yes, but only because it's for a good cause. I'm still mad at you." She waved with her back turned as the door shut behind her.

Lena wandered around her house aimlessly, thinking. While part of her really wanted to get to know Amy on a more intimate level, she considered Amy's occupation and who she represented. She wasn't sure if that was fair, if she was being too judgmental, or if it was good sense taking over for her. Something inside her told her Amy could be trusted, but was it true? Could someone who protected people who'd done crappy, if not illegal, things actually be trusted? Her concern was Laura, and Laura's well-being. Nothing else mattered, and opening their lives to someone who might have suspect ethics wasn't a good idea. She had made the right choice by not inviting her to the restaurant tonight. She got up and headed to her shower. *It's the right choice. I know it.* She sighed. *So why does it bother me?*

Amy scrolled through the numbers in her phone. She needed to get out of her apartment, but finding someone who was free the night before Christmas Eve was proving to be more difficult than she had anticipated. There were three women Amy saw rather regularly, in order to keep her libido in check. All three wanted the same thing from her she wanted from them: a distraction. There was no commitment, no hope for a future filled with brunches and family dinners. Her connections with these women were physical, nothing more, and that was the way it needed to be. She came to Brittany's name and hesitated. Banishing Lena from her thoughts this way might not be terribly healthy. She was pretty sure a therapist would tell her she was trying to avoid her feelings, and she should be processing what these desires and emotions, things she hadn't felt for years, meant. *Fuck it.* She pushed the button, deciding to let fate decide.

Brittany was a photographer for the *San Francisco Chronicle.* She was bold, passionate, and exquisite. A thick, gravelly voice came through the speaker. "Amy. I haven't heard from you in about three months. To what do I owe this phone call?"

Amy, who normally swooned at the cool, dismissive way Brittany arranged her distinctive attitude, fought back an eye roll. "Just wanted to see what you were up to tonight?"

"In other words, you miss me."

Amy shook her head. "Modest as ever."

"Just making an observation, darlin'. I'll pick you up in fifteen minutes."

For a moment, she almost changed her mind, but she couldn't think of a good reason why. "Okay, see you then." Amy glanced down at her clothes. She would have normally changed for a date of this kind, but she decided her jeans and black V-neck shirt were good enough. She wouldn't be in them long anyway. She pulled her leather jacket out of the closet and headed to the elevator, letting her hair out of its ponytail on the way down. *A distraction is exactly what I need. Brittany is an excellent distraction.*

Amy heard the motorcycle before it pulled up to the curb. Brittany flipped open her visor, and her eyes smiled. Those aqua blue eyes. Amy used to think that she had never seen anything so blue, so beautiful, and so sexy. *Lena's are nicer.* Brittany's eyes were hard, a little dangerous, and always alluring. There was something different in Lena's eyes, though. They were welcoming, warm, and kind. Amy took the helmet from Brittany's outstretched hand, put it on, and climbed on the back of the bike.

"I need to go take a couple of pictures for one of my coworkers. I'm filling in for her tonight. It should only take about fifteen minutes, some fluff piece."

Amy wrapped her arms around Brittany's body, and tried not to compare it to the thought of Lena's. "Yeah, that's fine."

The bike slipped through the glowing streets, rarely slowing for any obstacles. Brittany simply glided around them, the motorcycle an extension of her body. The ride was exhilarating and exactly what Amy needed in order to take her mind off Lena. The vibrations of the bike and her closeness to another human were comforting. The buildings became less frequent and the cold grasp of the ocean air was constant, even through the leather jacket. The bike slowed, and Amy's heart beat erratically when they took the left turn onto Geary Street. *Lands End.* Brittany parked the bike and turned the key, leaving the powerful engine quiet. She reversed her position, still straddling the bike, but facing Amy. Amy pulled off her helmet and smiled. Brittany didn't need to know her excitement had nothing to do with Brittany. She was going to see Lena again, in just a few short moments. Brittany pushed the tussled hair out of Amy's face, tucking it behind her ear. She put her palms on Amy's knees and pushed them up her legs, stopping at the bottom of Amy's zipper.

"I promise this will only take a few minutes."

Amy nodded. There was a lump in the back of her throat and a feeling of guilt traipsing through her subconscious. She suddenly had a thought, a thought that kept her unable to move from her seat. She didn't want Lena to think she was "with" Brittany, nor did she want to explain that Brittany was someone she used to extinguish her sexual needs. It really, really mattered to her that Lena didn't see her as shallow. *Even if it's true?* Brittany pulled her out of her internal reflection. She grabbed Amy's ass and pulled her forward on the bike before she draped Amy's legs over her own and kissed along her jawline. Amy's heart was racing. Brittany had that effect on, well, every woman within a fifteen-foot radius of her. But along with that effect was just an edge of panic, of the desire to run.

Amy placed her hands on Brittany's chest and pushed her back. "Let's go get this taken care of so we can get out of here."

Brittany flashed the smile that usually had Amy ready to rip her clothes off. Now…she just wanted to get out of there before Lena saw them together. *Since when have I been ashamed of who I am?*

❖

Lena moved a flower arrangement for what she was pretty sure was the thousandth time, give or take. Lilies. They were her mom's favorite, and they decorated every table, just as they did on every twenty-third of every month. Lena had decided to start this tradition about a month after she had taken over Lands End. The homeless population of San Francisco was one of the highest in the country, third only to New York and Los Angeles. Feeding them once a month wasn't going to fix the problem, but it was something. Lena rested easy in the knowledge that it was something they could count on, every month, without fail. Her parents would have been proud.

Laura came in, looking hurried. She glanced around the dining area, and once her gaze finally landed on Lena, she hurried over. "Where do you need me?"

Lena looked her little sister over, her gut telling her something was off. "Where were you?"

Laura rolled her eyes, an action Lena was starting to think was biologically required for teenagers before their brains allowed them to respond.

"I was at Marcy's."

"Did you go anywhere else?" Lena had been at Lands End since about three o'clock this afternoon, and hadn't heard from Laura during that time.

Laura crossed her arms. "No, Mom." Laura purposely dragged out the vowel.

Lena took a deep breath, trying to compose herself. "Just go cover the salad station. I'll deal with you later."

Laura rolled her eyes again. Thankfully, she stomped off to the salad station. Lena watched, amazed she could be so callous and then fifteen feet later be making pleasant conversation with the staff.

Chloe walked up beside her. "She does love you."

Lena was still watching her sister. "I don't know about that."

Chloe bumped her side. "Come on! Don't you remember when we were that age?"

Lena laughed. "That's exactly what I'm afraid of."

Chloe squeezed her arm. "Touché." Chloe looked around. "Everything looks great, by the way. Just like it always does."

"Thank you. I want everything to be perfect."

Chloe kissed her cheek. "It is, Lee. Where do you want me tonight?"

Lena looked around. "Wherever you want."

"Okay. I'll be at the bar."

Lena was walking toward the kitchen. "Fine, but you pay tonight."

Chloe stomped her foot and yelled after her. "Forget it then. Slave driver."

❖

Brittany pulled her camera bag out of the satchel attached to the side of her bike. She was looking through her equipment, clearly doing her job, but Amy felt like a kid on Christmas morning, kind of. She wanted to run inside and see Lena, and yet, the other part of her wanted to get away as quickly as possible.

Brittany glanced up as she continued to arrange her lenses. "Don't look so anxious. Like I said, this won't take long."

Amy rubbed her arms to fight off the night chill and to squelch her nerves a little. "No, it's fine. I've actually met the woman that runs the place."

Brittany stopped what she was doing and looked up. "You know Lena Michaels?"

Amy wasn't sure if she should've said anything, but it was too late now. "Yes, I had to have a meeting with her because of a work situation."

Brittany looked confused. "What could Lena Michaels have done that she required *you*?"

Amy felt a little hurt, and a little defensive, about her chosen profession. She knew her reply was going to come off harsher than intended, but she couldn't help it. "She didn't need to hire me. It was a different issue altogether. Nothing I can talk about, especially to you."

Brittany apparently realized she had injured Amy's feelings. She put a hand on Amy's shoulder, and her tone softened. "I didn't mean to imply anything. I was just surprised. I read all the information we have on her family and this place after I offered to fill in. It was an incredible story."

Amy was still irritated. She knew she had no valid reason to be, but that didn't change the fact that she was. "I thought you said this was a fluff piece? And since when are you the one asking the questions? I thought we were here to take pictures."

Brittany slung her bag over her shoulder and started walking toward the front doors of Lands End. "My degree is actually in journalism. I've only done small pieces for the paper, but I think this might be my chance to prove I can do more. The assignment is this event, but I don't think that's where the real story is. She does this every single month on the twenty-third. She closes it down to regular patrons and opens it to feed as many homeless people as possible. She's done it for the last six years and keeps it quiet. We only found out because we were doing an interview at a homeless shelter regarding the holidays. I think the real story is the murder of her parents, the case never being solved, and where she and her sister are now."

Amy was disappointed with herself. She'd spent countless hours with Brittany and had never known she had a passion for journalism, much less a degree in it. *Is it possible I'm that shallow?* Regardless of Amy's inattention, Brittany was correct, the public loved hard luck stories, but she knew Lena wouldn't want that kind of intrusion, and she felt irrationally protective of her. Lena didn't need her protection, but that didn't stop her. "I seriously doubt she's going to answer your questions. She seems like a pretty private person, and I don't think she'll want her sister involved at all."

Brittany stopped before she opened the door. "Will you introduce me? She might be more comfortable if I'm here with someone she knows. And we didn't have time to call her, since this is kind of a last-minute addition."

Amy didn't know what to say. There was no valid reason she shouldn't, but she damn sure didn't want to. Brittany was staring at her, and Amy could feel her skin flushing, but this time it was with irritation. "We'll see what happens."

Lena was going through her mental checklist. There was soup, bread, salad, chicken, roasted vegetables, and a table of boxed lunches so everyone could have food for the next day as well. There were crates of bottled water stacked high. During the winter months, she also put out as many blankets as she could procure, either through donations or purchasing them herself. The doors would be open momentarily, and she would keep them open until everyone was fed. They had never turned anyone away if there were still people wanting. She walked over to the window and looked out at the black water. She couldn't see the impressive Pacific Ocean at this time of night, but the reflection of the living city in the glimmer on the water brought her peace. The water, these windows, the sparkles of light— they were the same that her mother visited reverently, and Lena loved to replicate it. The closeness she felt was fleeting, but worth it.

A staff member walked up behind her. "There's someone from the *San Francisco Chronicle* here to see you."

Lena was surprised and worried. Worried for Laura, and unsure if her recent escapades had been revealed. She turned around. "Do you know what for?"

He shook his head. "She didn't say. Would you like me to find out?"

Lena thought about it for a moment before she answered. "No. I'll take care of it." She headed for the front of the restaurant, already determined to put the reporter in their place.

Chapter Six

Amy watched Brittany snap what must have been a thousand pictures. She was moving along the line that had formed at the front of Lands End. Amy couldn't guess how many people there were. Hundreds of tattered San Franciscans waited, rubbing their arms and hands trying to stay warm. She silently berated herself. She knew it was a problem in her city, but she didn't realize how big of an issue it was until faced with it, here and now. There were people of all shapes and sizes, all ages, all ethnicities. This issue didn't discriminate; it seemed to just consume. Several families huddled closely together, and Amy wondered what circumstances had placed them here. What surprised Amy was that some of the children ran around and carried on as if they didn't have a care in the world. The harsh realization that some of them probably didn't know any other way of life gripped Amy's heart and squeezed.

"Amy? What are you doing here?" *Lena.* She sounded angry and a bit unsettled.

Amy turned around. Lena looked perfect. She stood a foot from her, her red button-down shirt perfectly pressed, just a bit snug around the arms and breasts. Her hair was tucked behind her ears, and her blue eyes shimmered. Amy was worried they would be swirling with anger, but that's not what she saw. *Kindness and warmth.* Her tone might have been angry, but she still looked…sweet. Amy shook herself. *Reply, dummy. Like a normal human being.*

She was about to string a coherent sentence together when Brittany showed up beside her. "Hi, Lena. I'm Brittany O'Brien from the *San Francisco Chronicle*."

Brittany put out her hand and Lena took it. "Nice to meet you, Brittany. What can I help you with this evening?" Lena's tone was calm, but Amy knew instinctively she wasn't.

"We'd like to do a piece on what you do here every month for the homeless. It's very impressive. I'll just be taking a few pictures tonight, but I'd like to contact you for an interview when you aren't so busy."

Lena looked at Amy, and her expression softened slightly. Amy felt a twinge of guilt at the realization that Lena had thought she'd brought Brittany here because of her sister.

"I'm not interested in doing any interviews. This has never been, and never will be, for publicity."

Brittany nodded but kept pushing. "I completely understand. But, Lena, this is a good thing you're doing here."

Lena crossed her arms. "I'm not interested. These people suffer enough, and now you want to exploit them for a story? I won't do that to them."

Brittany seemed to contemplate this for a minute. "Don't think of it as exploiting them. Think of it as helping them."

"How would a story showing them at some of their weakest and hardest moments help them?"

Brittany had clearly anticipated the question. "It shows what an epidemic homelessness really is in our city. If other people see that a restaurant like Lands End is willing to do something like this every month, who knows the effect it will have? You might inspire more business owners to help, or cause a surge of donations. They might even have job offers for some of these people. And it could let other homeless people who don't know about it, find you. I have no intention of exploiting anyone. Maybe we could help you make it bigger, a movement of sorts."

Lena uncrossed her arms and looked out over the growing line. "You really think that would happen?"

Brittany nodded. "I do. The power of something like this could be incredible, if only other people knew about it."

Lena seemed to consider it. "Then please focus on them. This isn't about me, and I don't want to see any pictures of myself or my sister."

Amy could tell Brittany didn't like the answer by the long breath she exhaled. "That isn't ideal, but okay. You'll still do the interview, though?"

Lena nodded and took a step backward, no longer blocking the front doors. "Welcome to Lands End."

Lena walked from table to table. She tried her best to talk to everyone that came in, but it was a futile act, and she knew she missed dozens of people every time, but it was also something she felt was imperative. She wanted all of these people, if even for just one night of the month, to feel like normal customers. She wanted them to feel like part of society, not pariahs. She placed a flyer for the few job openings she had available on each of the tables. Throughout all of her conversations, she still managed to keep an eye on Amy and her friend. She had a lot of questions, and didn't know if they were appropriate to ask. Starting with who was Brittany to her, and why was she with her tonight?

Lena walked over to the salad station where both Laura and Chloe were busy filling plates. "How are you two holding up?"

Laura pulled an empty tray from the serving table and replaced it with another from the cart behind her. "Great. We're really busy tonight."

Lena agreed. It always pleased her that Laura genuinely enjoyed helping on these nights. It gave her hope that her sweet little sister was still somewhere in there, and she wouldn't be held captive by this teenager forever. "Yes, we are. It's a great turnout."

Laura continued. "Do you need help at the blanket station? We're almost done here."

Lena glanced over and saw two staff members were already there. "No, they seem to have it covered. If you'd like though, you can help me do some of the meet and greets."

Laura's face lit up. "Really? You've never let me do that before."

Lena placed her hand on her back. "Yes. I think you're old enough now not to embarrass us."

Laura rolled her eyes but smiled anyway. "Okay. Thanks, Lena."

Chloe pushed her out of the way. "Go take off that apron and fix your hair. You look like a hot mess."

Laura quickly disappeared back into the staff area. Chloe moved the salad trays around so she could do the serving herself. The line had died down, but people were still sporadically coming up to fill, or refill, their plates. Lena could tell Chloe had something on her mind. "What?"

Chloe looked up. "What, what?"

Lena sighed. "Just ask, Chloe."

Chloe kept moving things around on the table. "I was just curious as to why Amy Kline is here with a reporter."

Lena watched Amy, who had offered to help pass out boxed lunches. They kept making eye contact, and each time they did, Lena's heart sped up. She wasn't going to tell Chloe that though, not yet. "I don't know why they're here together."

Chloe took a side step closer to Lena. "Don't you think you should ask her?"

Lena considered Chloe's question. Amy had long ago removed her leather jacket. Her T-shirt was one you could find in the Haight-Ashbury, an old band name from the sixties clinging to her chest, and just short enough that every time she turned around to pick up more boxes, Lena could see the small of her back. Her hair was pulled back out of her face, and when she leaned forward on the table to talk to a little girl, her triceps were just barely visible, even from this distance. Lena fought the urge to go over and touch her. "No, I don't need to ask her. It's none of my business."

"Uh huh. No. Of course it's not. There is absolutely no reason why you should be curious as to why the woman you were practically on top of this morning, who also happens to be the same woman handling your little sister's episode with a twenty-something married football player, is in your restaurant with a reporter. Makes perfect sense."

Lena pulled her gaze away from Amy for a moment. "I was not practically on top of her."

Chloe rolled her eyes. "That's what you took from that, huh?"

Lena moved away from the table. "Okay, Chloe. I'll go talk to her. Just for you."

Chloe nodded decisively and turned to the person waiting for food. "Yeah, okay, good. Go."

Amy watched Lena come closer, her stride purposeful and intent. Intent on her, apparently, and it made her skin tingle. Amy had flashes of being the complete focus of someone with that much passion, determination, and that all-consuming gaze. She needed to swallow, breathe…something. Lena made it to the table, and Amy felt it again. The connectivity, the electricity that pulsed between them, it wasn't like anything she had ever experienced. The side of Lena's mouth turned up just slightly, revealing a partial smile.

"Can I talk to you for a minute?"

"Of course."

Lena looked around and started to walk toward the corner of the room. Amy came from behind the table and followed her. Lena turned down the hallway and made it to the end. The doorplate identified it as her office. Lena pushed the door open and walked in, and Amy followed, trying not to stare at her perfect ass.

"I need to ask you a question." Lena leaned against her desk, her hands gripping the top tightly, and Amy noticed her knuckles were white. Lena was either nervous or angry. Amy hoped it was the first.

"Okay, what's up?"

"Who is Brittany and why are you here with her?"

Amy hadn't been prepared to answer the question. As usual, Lena had caught her off guard. Of course, she should've come up with an answer to the obvious query as soon as she'd realized they were going to Lands End. She just hadn't managed to think beyond the anticipation of seeing Lena. "She's a friend of mine, and when she picked me up tonight, she said she needed to come do an assignment. I had no idea it was here until I arrived. My being here has nothing to do with Laura. It's just a bizarre coincidence."

Lena seemed to consider the answer before she spoke again. "Just a friend?"

Amy felt a lump in her throat at the lie forming. Brittany was a friend, but she didn't think that was what Lena was implying. Nor was she about to confirm the real nature of their friendship. "If you're asking if I'm dating Brittany, the answer is no."

Lena nodded. She reached out and grabbed Amy's hands, pulling her closer. Amy stood between Lena's legs, and with her partially sitting on the desk, they were the same height. "It's okay if you are dating her. I just wanted to know the situation and to make sure it had nothing to do with my sister. I like to know where I stand. I need to understand."

The words made sense in Amy's head, but she was having difficulty stringing them all together. She was only inches from Lena's lips. She caught the faint whiff of Lena's perfume as she leaned closer, wanting to take her in. She watched Lena's jaw tighten and then relax again. Amy tried to think back to a time where she had found jaw movement sexy, and unsurprisingly, there wasn't one. Amy thought how fortunate she was that her body knew how to keep her breathing, standing upright, and balanced, because she wouldn't have been able to do any of it on her own.

Amy wrapped her arms around Lena's neck and watched her perfect blue eyes once again focus on her mouth. She wasn't going to, couldn't, wait any longer. She leaned forward and pressed her lips into Lena's rewarding, soft, vanilla-laced, waiting mouth. Lena's shoulders shifted under her arms and she pulled Amy closer. The closeness was intoxicating. Amy had kissed dozens, if not a hundred, women in her life, and not a single one of them was anything like this. She felt it in every part of her body. The kiss made her tingle, set her on fire, and calmed her all at the same time. Lena's hands wrapped around her waist and clung to her sides. Each movement sent exhilarating chills through her body. Lena softly bit Amy's bottom lip and then pulled away. Her cheeks were flushed and her eyes were a bit hazy.

"I need to go back out there," Lena said.

Amy nodded silently because words escaped her completely.

Lena seemed to complete her thought. "I don't want to go back out there."

Amy slid her hands from behind Lena's neck and ran them down her arms until she reached her hands. "Then don't."

Lena chewed on her bottom lip, seeming to ponder the idea. It was unbelievably sexy, especially because she didn't seem to realize she was doing it. Amy leaned closer again. She ran her lips down Lena's jawline, ending at her chin. Lena's breath was at her ear, and it felt as if someone was breathing life into her. Lena was absolutely exquisite.

Lena stood, breaking their closeness. "I really do need to be out there."

Amy was disappointed, but she didn't want to let it show. "Yes, of course."

Lena walked to the door and pulled it open for Amy to exit. Amy walked by and squeezed Lena's hand as she passed. The pressure she felt in the return was reassuring.

Once in the hallway, Brittany was upon them. "There you are."

Amy nodded, hoping she didn't look as guilty as she felt. "Here I am."

Brittany looked back and forth between Lena and Amy. Her facial expression said she knew something was going on between them. She looked at them with an eyebrow raised. "I'm all finished up here, if you want to get going."

Amy, still unable to put sentences together, simply nodded. Brittany looked at Lena. "I'd still like to get that interview. Are you available on the twenty-sixth?"

Lena pulled out her phone. "Let me just double-check my schedule."

Amy felt like she was stuck in a time warp. It had only been a few seconds, but standing between Lena and Brittany, trying to pretend like that kiss hadn't just happened, was excruciating.

"I'll be out of town starting tomorrow and returning the afternoon of the twenty-sixth. I can be available at around four o'clock that day, if that works for you."

Brittany jotted down the information on her notepad. "Yes, that's perfect. Meet here, then?"

Lena smiled at them. "That'll be fine. I hope you both have a lovely holiday." She turned and walked into the dining area, her smile ready for her patrons.

Brittany already had all of her gear packed and in her bag. She was holding Amy's coat. Amy watched Lena walk away and aimlessly reached for the jacket.

"You okay?"

Nope. Not okay. Not okay at all. Her head was still spinning from that kiss. "Yeah, I'm good. Ready to go?"

Brittany looked at her suspiciously. "Yeah, okay."

They walked into the parking lot. The cold night air was invigorating. It felt like a cool spray on a hot summer day, and Amy's skin was just that, hot. It still burned from Lena's touch, Lena's stare. Brittany put her things back into the side satchel, and Amy grabbed the helmet she had used earlier that night, getting ready to put it back on.

"You want to go back to my place?"

Amy looked at Brittany, and for the first time since meeting her, felt nothing. There was no pull, no need. Brittany was gorgeous, mysterious, and fabulous in bed. She also no longer had any allure. Amy shook her head. "Nah. I'm pretty tired. Can you just take me home?"

Brittany climbed on her bike, a knowing grin on her lips. "No problem."

"Where were you?"

Lena was watching Laura who was sitting at a table, talking to a family that was there every month. She glanced up at Chloe. "I was in my office."

"Yes. Thank you for over sharing. I watched you two walk into your office."

Lena was still watching her sister. "Then why did you ask?"

"Are we really going to do this? Where I ask you the same question a thousand different ways until you finally tell me what I actually want to know? And don't act like you aren't going to tell me. You always tell me. Spill."

Lena loved aggravating Chloe. "They aren't dating, and she didn't even know she was coming here tonight. So it wasn't about Laura."

"And that needed to be discussed in your office with the door shut?"

Lena patted Chloe on the back before she stood to go to Laura. "I couldn't very well kiss her out here in front of you."

❖

A few hours later, Lena lay in the darkness of her bedroom. The ticking cadence from the old clock that sat in the corner of her room usually lulled her to sleep. Tonight, it was an annoyance instead of a comfort. She couldn't dispel the image of Amy from her mind. The way she felt, the way she smelled. Her senses seemed to still be swimming in her remnants. She didn't know how she felt about what had happened between them. Well, that wasn't entirely true. She knew how her body felt about Amy—the lightness in her stomach and the hot flush she felt just remembering kissing her lips was apparent. Her mind was an entirely different story. Lena wanted to trust Amy's intentions. She wanted to believe what she said was true, but should she? Amy was a contradiction. She seemed genuine, caring, and sweet, but how could someone who was all of those things still do what they do for a living?

The draw of sleep was finally starting to tug at her subconscious. Her thoughts became a bit more jumbled, with bits of blankness. Right before she finally gave in, the last image of Amy flashed through her mind. It wasn't apprehension that Lena fell asleep to; it was hope.

CHAPTER SEVEN

L aura! We need to get going! It's only two nights. Let's go!" Yelling up the staircase had become a habit, one Lena wasn't thrilled with. It made her feel old and very mom-like. She dragged out the last few wrapped presents and put them in the trunk of her car.

"Why do we have to go? Can't we just stay here?"

Lena closed the trunk. "No, we go up to Chloe's parents' every year. It's not like you're missing time with your friends. They all have to be with their families, too."

Laura threw her bag into the backseat. "Lena, there's like, zero reception up there. It's barbaric."

Lena ran up the front steps and double-checked to make sure the front door was locked. She got into the driver's seat and then answered Laura. "You aren't going to die. Who knows, you may even have a little bit of fun. I brought Apples to Apples. Plus, you can still text. You'll just have to catch up on Facebook, Twitter, Instagram, Tumblr, and whatever else I'm missing that keeps you overly connected to your friends. I'm sure you can find out what they all ate for Christmas dinner when we get back."

Laura latched her seat belt and leaned her head against the window. "Sounds horrific."

After one hundred and ninety-five miles, three gas station stops, seven arguments over the radio, and three pleas to turn around, they were finally in Lake Tahoe. The cabin had been in Chloe's family for years. It was located on a quiet street that backed up against the Truckee River. The majestic pine trees of Tahoe were outside every window and had just been dusted with a light snowfall. Expansions and upgrades had been made to the home over the years, but it still held its rustic charm.

Chloe came running out the front door and met them in the driveway. "You guys are finally here!"

Laura said sarcastically, "And we're ready to party."

Chloe patted Laura's head as she went by. "Your excitement is contagious, Laura. My brother should be here in a few hours, so you'll have someone to sulk around with."

Lena was pulling her bag and gifts from the trunk when Chloe was beside her.

"Hey, friend." Chloe annunciated the word "friend" like it had suddenly been reconfigured with four extra vowels that dragged on longer than necessary.

"You're obviously dying to ask me something."

Chloe grabbed the last bag out of the car and shut Lena's trunk. "Nope, just happy you two are here."

"Chloe, there isn't a whole lot else to tell you about last night."

Chloe's grin stretched from ear to ear. "HA! But there is *something* else to tell me."

Lena started walking up to the front door. "You're a crazy person."

Chloe followed quickly behind. "But I'm *your* crazy person, and I want details."

Lena was rescued by the emergence of Chloe's mother. "Knock it off, Chloe. Whatever you're doing to bug Lena, knock it off." Tina wrapped Lena in a welcoming hug. Chloe passed by mumbling and Lena kissed Tina's cheek.

"I missed you."

Tina placed both hands on Lena's face. "We missed you, too. Now, go inside and put your things down so we can catch up."

❖

"Please, just come. My mom makes the best stuffed chicken you've ever tasted." Sarah called to invite Amy to Christmas Eve dinner at her parents' house.

"I appreciate the offer, but I don't want to intrude on your family time." Amy walked over to her balcony window and watched as the cars drove by on the street below.

"Oh come on, you'd be doing me a favor. Matt is stuck at work, and I had to leave without him. You could give him a ride."

Amy looked down at her cardinal color sweatpants that boasted her alma mater down the leg in fading white letters. She had already resigned herself to the fact that she would be staying in for the holiday, and this was, without question, her preferred attire for such an occasion. But Sarah had different plans, and she wasn't going to take no for an answer. Persistence was one of her many superpowers. "Okay. I need an hour to get ready. Will Matt be ready by then?"

Amy could hear Sarah smiling. "I'll tell him he has to be."

Amy had already started walking into her bathroom. "Where should I pick him up?"

"If you could, the station would be easiest. He works down at the Richmond Station, on Sixth Avenue."

Amy turned on the water to her shower and regretfully started pulling off her beloved sweatpants. "Okay, see you in a bit."

Sarah caught her before she hung up. "Oh, and, Amy... we're a jeans kind of group."

Amy was thankful Sarah had disclosed that bit of information before she overdressed. "Got it, thanks."

An hour later, almost to the minute, Amy drove down Sixth Avenue to pick up Matt. She had barely applied any makeup and was in her favorite pair of jeans and the plum sweater she had worn the first day she had met Lena. *Lena.* Amy was surprised that her heart rate slightly increased at just the thought of her. Her mind started to wander. She unconsciously licked her bottom lip in a futile and impossible attempt to taste her again. Amy felt chills run up her arms and across her neck as she replayed the kiss in her mind. She was so lost in the memory, she didn't realize she had missed the station altogether until the woman on the navigation system told her to make a U-turn. *Geez. Bossy.*

Matt was waiting at the curb and got in as soon as Amy pulled up. He shut the door and rubbed his arms. "I have no idea how people live in the snow." He blew into his hands.

Amy cocked her head and laughed. "I assure you they wear more than a polo shirt on Christmas Eve in other parts of the country."

Matt grinned. "Touché."

Amy had only met Matt a handful of times, but she didn't need much more than that to know she genuinely liked him. He had an openness about him not many people possessed. He was easy to talk to, engaging, and had a boyish sense of humor without being immature.

Traffic was light going out of the city and they made it to the 101 in record time. They were catching up with light conversation when Amy's phone rang. It was enabled to the Bluetooth automatically when she got in the car, so Amy assumed it would be Sarah. She had already talked to Addison earlier that day, her parents would call tomorrow, and no one else would be calling her on Christmas Eve. She didn't bother to check the name on the caller ID as she pushed the talk button on her steering wheel. "Hello?"

"Amy, hi."

Amy paused. It wasn't Sarah.

"Hi, Brittany. I have you on speaker. I'm in the car with a friend of mine. What's up?" Amy quietly panicked. She hoped that her mention of being on speaker would prevent her from mentioning anything taboo.

"I was calling about Lena Michaels."

Amy quickly processed. *First and last name. So, a professional call.* "Okay, what about her?"

"I pitched the story to my editor, and we both think the real story is with the unsolved murders."

Amy dealt with stories for a living. Spinning them, changing them, manipulating them, but this made her uneasy. "I don't understand what that has to do with me, Brittany."

"Well, she may need some convincing."

"And what makes you think I'm the person for that undertaking?"

"I've seen the way she looks at you. And if there's anyone on the planet who can convince people to do what she wants them to, it's you."

Amy briefly glanced over at Matt, who was obviously trying to make it seem like he wasn't listening by looking out the window and tapping a random beat on his leg. "I've met her a handful of times. If you want this interview, you need to ask her."

"I plan on it. Can you just put in a good word for me if it comes up, push her in my direction?"

"You aren't going to portray her or her sister in a negative light, right?"

Brittany scoffed. "Of course not! From everything I can tell, they're good people and you never know, this may help. Someone could come forward with information."

The pit was growing larger in Amy's stomach. "We'll see."

Brittany seemed satisfied. "That's all I can ask. Thank you, and happy holidays."

"You too." Amy ended the call.

The car was silent, but Amy's mind was bouncing in a hundred different directions. Matt broke her internal reflection.

"I don't mean to butt in, but were you two talking about the Bradley and Michelle Michaels murders?"

Amy wasn't surprised he had put the pieces together. *He's a detective, for Christ's sake.* "Yes. Well, more specifically, we were talking about Lena and Laura Michaels."

Matt shook his head. "That's one where we still beat our heads against a wall. Damn shame what happened to that family. Those poor girls." Matt seemed genuinely bothered.

"Do you know a lot about it?"

"Only what I've read in the case files. We review a lot of cold cases going through detective training. A nine-year-old as the only witness doesn't give us a lot of traction." He paused, looking thoughtful. "Your friend wants to do a story?"

Amy nodded. "She works for the *Times*. Do you think it would help?"

Matt was silent for a moment. "It wouldn't be the first time re-examining a case brought new things to light. But it can take its toll on the people involved. Opens old wounds, for no reason."

Amy didn't reply because she wasn't sure what she wanted more, to protect Lena from having to go through something like that, or to hope that she was able to get closure on something that had brought her family anguish for years. *Really, it's none of my business. She's not my responsibility. Right?*

Lena took a seat in her recliner. She called it her recliner because it was her favorite seat, not just at this particular house, but anywhere she had ever sat. Tina and David were moving around the kitchen with the kind of almost-choreographed simplicity only long-term couples could achieve. Chopping vegetables, checking the oven, singing along to the Christmas song classics they had on repeat. The couple was a well-oiled machine, and Lena loved it. Witnessing it should have made her miss her parents, but instead, she was grateful for Tina and David. Tina and her mother had been best friends since childhood, and their families had spent every Christmas together, in this cabin, for Lena's entire life. She was eternally grateful the tradition had never been altered. Even the year her parents had passed, Tina and David made sure both Lena and her sister were there with them. Lena could never express her appreciation for their genuine kindness. If even for a brief few days, their lives had felt normal and consistent.

Laura sat on the couch a few feet away. She was watching the pair in the kitchen, as well. She was smiling, but Lena didn't comment, knowing that the recognition of Laura's happiness would cause its quick disappearance. Lena closed her eyes briefly. The smell of cinnamon and the fire that burned next to her filled her senses. She suddenly wondered what Amy was doing. Was she alone or was she with friends? The thought of her being alone didn't sit well. She pulled out her phone and flipped to Amy's number, hitting the message button. "Hope you're having a good holiday. Thinking about you." Lena's thumb hovered over the little blue button.

"Just push send."

Lena looked at her sister, who was staring at her with a bored expression.

"What?"

Laura, in her annoyed voice, said, "Push send. You're over thinking it."

Lena wondered how she could possibly know what she was doing.

Laura sighed dramatically. "Amy…the girl from last night, right? Push send."

Lena pushed send and set the phone down. "How did you know?"

Laura shook her head. "Everyone who was within ten feet of you two would know who you were texting. You being you, you're probably over analyzing every word in that text."

"Since when did you start doling out relationship advice?"

Laura, who rarely missed a beat, answered after a moment of silence. "Since I haven't seen you smile the way you did last night in, I don't even know how long."

Before Lena had a chance to say another word, the front door swung open and cracked against the wall.

"I hope all you wanted was my attendance for Christmas, because I didn't bring anything else."

"Benjamin!" Tina's voice was filled with excitement and appreciation that her son had just walked through the door.

"Hi, Mom." He swung her around in a tight hug.

Benjamin, or Ben, had turned into a man overnight. She had seen him last Christmas, but the slightly awkward, gangly boy had grown up in the last three hundred and sixty-five days. The person that stood in his mom's embrace had filled out, had a five o'clock shadow, and had retired his ever-present Converse shoes. Ben hugged his dad and then turned his attention to the hallway, where Chloe came bounding out of the bathroom. The two greeted each other with a hug at first, which quickly transitioned into various botched hold attempts with bits of laughter sprinkled in.

Lena got out of her recliner and walked over to the eighteen-year-old who had followed her and Chloe around for as long as she could remember. He opened his arms and she stepped into his hug.

Ben gave hugs like his mom. "Hi, Lena," he whispered in her ear.

She kissed his cheek and stepped back, looking him up and down. "I can't believe the difference a year makes."

He rubbed his chest, obviously proud of his transformation. "I decided to take a few breaks from writing code this year and spent them at the gym."

Lena nodded. "I'll say."

Laura was beside her almost instantly. "Hi, Ben."

Ben hugged Laura. Lena briefly thought he was going to pick her up, the embrace lasted so long. David walked over and patted Ben on the back. Ben turned his attention away from Laura, and Lena caught a glimpse of Laura's face. She nudged Chloe to make sure she wasn't the only one taking inventory. Chloe rolled her eyes and grabbed his bag. "You're downstairs, across from me."

Ben turned and followed Chloe down the hall. "What? No bunk beds this year?"

Chloe glanced at Laura. "Don't tempt me."

CHAPTER EIGHT

The text message from Lena appeared on the navigation screen in Amy's car. Matt caught a glimpse and tried to hide his smile by turning to look out the window. Amy rolled her eyes. "The technology in this car is exposing my life to you."

Matt laughed, and Amy felt a little less embarrassed. "Amy, if you're worried about me knowing you're gay, I don't care."

Amy felt a little frazzled. "It's not that." She looked over at him, and though the car was dark, she could make out his facial features reflecting from the dashboard lights. "Although, I am a little bit startled that everyone knows. I've never tried to hide it, but I also didn't realize it was so obvious."

Matt patted her leg. "Do you remember Amber Brown? Or Melanie Jacobs?" Amy did, in fact, remember both of the women. "What about Rebecca Martin?"

Amy nodded and let out a long breath. She attempted a smile that was probably less than convincing. "Yes, of course I remember them. I'm also suddenly recalling that Amber and Melanie are police officers, and that Rebecca is a firefighter."

Matt smiled his charming, knowing smile. "It would be safe for you to assume you've been the topic of more than one conversation at parties."

Amy winced. "It was never my intention to hurt anyone."

Matt nodded. "I believe that. Everything I've heard from Sarah about you, I don't think you're that kind of person. I think each of them just thought they could be the one to settle you down. But they were clear that you always said you didn't want anything more. Doesn't stop them from hoping, though."

Amy was beyond relieved when the bossy voice on her navigation system informed them they were arriving at their destination. "We made it. Ready to spend the holiday with your potential in-laws?"

Matt's eyes widened as he reached for the handle. "Is anyone ever really ready for that?"

The house could have been an inspiration for a Thomas Kinkade painting. The lights were hung perfectly. Decorations were placed around the lawn in an obviously premeditated formation. It included Santa, his reindeer, even a rather large train set, and a nativity scene. There was a soft glow coming from the large front windows, where inside you could see people moving around. The trees were perfectly pruned, and the cobblestone path, which led to the front door, had a backdrop of subtle smoke emanating from the chimney. "It's a good thing you swooped in and saved Sarah from this dreary life she's been forced to live."

Matt put his hands in his pockets and stared at the house for a moment before he spoke. "I'll never be able to afford to give Sarah a house like this."

Amy put her hand on Matt's back as they started to walk to the front door. "Matt, I assure you, whether or not that's true has nothing to do with the way Sarah feels about you. She loves you."

Matt tilted his head. "I'm not sure her dad feels the same."

Amy knocked on the door. "I'm sure he just wants his daughter to be happy. And you do make her happy."

Sarah pulled the door open, and the music and laughter poured out from behind her. It was clear this family loved

Christmas. The warmth she could feel immediately stuck to her, like mist on a foggy morning, and she loved it. Amy thought of Addison, on assignment away from everything comforting and holiday infused. Sarah broke up her thoughts with a warm hug and a kiss on the cheek. She grabbed the bottle of wine out of Amy's hand and looked down at the label. "Red, perfect."

Matt smiled at the love of his life. "Hey, gorgeous."

Sarah kissed him. "Hi, Matty." She grabbed his hand and pulled him inside. Amy followed.

Amy excused herself to the restroom, which Sarah directed her to. White walls with black-and-white photographs lined the hallway; Sarah, her two older brothers, and their parents, all in various stages of life and portraying different levels of bliss. It made Amy smile and feel just a touch of sadness at being without her own family this year. She reached the bathroom and shut the door quickly behind her. She pulled out her phone. She couldn't wait to actually read the text from Lena. She hadn't been expecting to hear from her at all, and saying it was a pleasant surprise was a ridiculous understatement.

Hope you're having a good holiday. Thinking about you.

Amy's stomach flipped as she tapped the phone against her chin. She felt that familiar flush rush through her cheeks as it usually did when she thought of Lena. Amy tapped the text box, and the curser started to blink. Her typical response would be to wait several hours, if not a day, to return a text that indicated any type of emotional interest. She was the queen of playing it cool. It wasn't a title she'd earned overnight. It had taken her years to perfect the art of keeping someone at arm's length, but close enough to keep their interest until it became too serious or had the potential to get messy. And yet…she didn't want to do that with Lena. She hadn't stopped thinking about her and wondered what she had been doing all day. *I miss her.* It was a silly thought, to miss someone she barely knew, someone she'd shared one kiss with. But she did. She looked back down at the blinking cursor. She willed her fingers to contribute something of substance, because her brain had apparently decided it didn't want to participate in lucid communication when it came to Lena. *Screw it.* "When can I see you again?" She hit send. It was too late to take it back. Amy was disappointed in herself. *Women like Lena need to be called and asked out, not sent messages like a teenager.* But texts weren't retrievable once she hit that stupid little button. *And neither is my dignity.* Amy gave herself a dirty look in the mirror, when her phone vibrated in her hand. The lump in her throat grew as she turned the phone over in her hand, and the mere second it took to complete that action felt like an eternity.

See me? You know where to find me.

Amy grinned at the response. *Playful is good.* Amy's thumbs hovered over the keyboard as she tried to think of a response that would be even slightly redeemable.

I would have called, but I didn't know if you were busy. I'd like to see you. Without work or coincidence.

She read it over before pushing send, checking for typos or an autocorrect mishap that could possibly infer an embarrassing sexual act. She nodded, and off the little message went. She watched her phone, those little blinking ellipses building her anticipation. She felt like she was waiting for her first crush to respond. *I'm ridiculous.*

Meet me at Lands End at eight o'clock on the twenty-sixth.

Amy smiled and did a small hopping dance in the bathroom. She quickly wrote back, *I can't wait,* and continued with her dance.

A knock on the bathroom door stopped her bouncing. "Amy, are you okay?"

Amy froze in place. "Yes, be out in a second."

❖

Chloe handed Lena a glass of eggnog and sat next to her on the couch, putting her head on Lena's shoulder. The fire was warm and comforting. Lena took a sip of the eggnog and tried to hold in her cough. "Who's pouring the rum this year?"

Chloe patted her leg. "Me."

Lena took another sip. "I should have figured." They sat in comfortable silence for a few more moments. "I'm going to see Amy again when I get back."

Chloe didn't move her head. "I figured."

"How did you figure?"

"I know you. You don't typically go off into your office to make out with girls."

"We were not making—" Lena stopped herself. "Are you just trying to see if there was something I left out, when I told you what happened?" She could feel Chloe's smile. "You're good."

Chloe sat up and faced her. "Are you sure this is something you want to pursue?"

"Weren't you the one telling me I need to meet someone?"

"Yes. But I'm not sure about *this* someone. Her involvement with the football player and Laura worries me."

"I changed Laura's number. They aren't communicating. Amy had nothing to do with that, anyway. And if I remember correctly, it was you that pointed that out to me the other night."

"No, but she protects his reputation by buying people off. It's her job. And of course I remember pointing that out to you; I thought you should give her the benefit of the doubt. People's jobs don't define them, but I also didn't realize at the time, you were thinking about dating her."

Lena didn't say anything for a moment. "He's not in the picture anymore. I told Laura she couldn't see him anymore."

"Oh! I didn't realize you had told her that. Well, then there should be no issue."

"Your sarcasm is noted."

"Just be careful. The woman lies and spins stories for a living. I don't think it's just a coincidence she had a reporter there with her last night."

Lena took another sip of her Chloe strength eggnog. "You lie for a living and I still spend time with you."

Chloe's eyes got big. "I do not!"

"You're a lawyer."

"I protect people's rights. Everyone deserves a fair trial."

"Then why don't you give her one? Innocent until proven guilty, right?"

"I see what you did there. Maybe you should have been the lawyer."

"Then where would you eat for free?"

Chloe let out a long sigh and rubbed her belly. "Good point."

Tina and David walked into the living room holding a stack of wrapped boxes. She yelled for Laura and Ben, who came into the room moments later. Tina handed a box to everyone. She had done this every Christmas for their entire lives.

Chloe took hers. "I wonder what this is." She shook the box next to her ear for dramatic flair. "Could it be pajamas?"

Tina gave Chloe a warning look. "Chloe, one day I'm going to skip you and you'll get nothing Christmas Eve."

Chloe smiled at her mom. "I'm just kidding, Mom. I know it's one of your favorite traditions."

Lena chimed in. "Don't let her fool you, Tina. She wears the pajamas all year long. We would never hear the end of it if this tradition ever stopped."

A few minutes later, the living room looked like a paper shredder had been possessed by an evil deity and let loose, leaving nothing but tattered wrapping and flimsy cardboard boxes in its wake. Everyone held up their yearly prized pajamas to show one another. Tina watched on, the glow on her face indicating her pure excitement. Everyone made the rounds of kissing Tina's cheek and thanking her.

Clothes were changed immediately after. Everyone donned their new flannel pajamas, which came in a variety of colors. Chloe's were pink, just as they were every year. Lena had a nice shade of blue. David and Ben had matching red and black. Laura's were the only pair that were completely different, with tiny pink dogs and cats dancing across the material. Lena knew it wasn't particularly her sister's taste, but she was gracious anyway. There was only one thing left to do to complete the annual tradition. David put a few more logs on the fire while Lena and Chloe refilled everyone's eggnog. Laura and Ben were both given hot chocolate that had been prepared in the Crockpot. Chloe took her normal seat next to Lena, and Tina curled up into David. The difference this year as the opening sequence for *Christmas Vacation* illuminated the screen was that Laura didn't sit in front of Lena on the floor. She sat next to Ben. *A little too close to Ben.* Chloe noticed too, and gave her a look that indicated she should let it go for the evening, so she did.

Amy sat in the midst of a whirlwind of laughter, good spirited inside jokes, and a variety of opinions on the latest political candidates. She didn't say much, not because she didn't feel welcome or thought anyone would have shunned her, but simply because she was enjoying listening too much. Sarah's brothers would be arriving the following day with their wives, and Amy was a little bit sad she was going to miss them, based on the stories her parents and aunts and uncles were telling. It was obvious Sarah was the baby of the family, and her brothers spent her entire life equally doting on her and harassing her. She managed a half glance over at Matt and felt a little sorry for him. Marrying the baby girl of this family would be no easy undertaking, and he knew it.

Matt's phone rang, and he excused himself from the table. Amy watched Sarah's reaction. She could read people better than almost anyone she had ever met, and that was part of what made her good at her job. The quiet sigh meant she knew this phone call marked the end of the evening for her boyfriend. Matt would need to leave. Amy didn't know if it was disappointment or worry changing Sarah's demeanor.

Clark, Sarah's dad, interrupted Amy's internal thought process. "Amy, I'm so glad you could join us this evening. It has been a pleasure finally meeting you. Sarah talks about you like you hung the moon."

Amy smiled, catching a glimpse of Sarah shaking her head out of the corner of her eye. "Thank you. And thank you for inviting me to share Christmas Eve with you and your family."

"For the life of me, I can't understand why Sarah hasn't brought you around sooner. You should meet her cousin Jim. He's single. And a doctor."

"Dad. Don't."

He sipped his brandy. "What? He is."

Amy laughed. "That's quite a compliment, but I assure you, Jim isn't my type."

Sarah's mom put her hand on her husband's arm, and Amy assumed Sarah and her mother had probably already had this exact conversation, but no one filled Clark in.

"How about some dessert, Clark?"

It was clear she had perfected this particular tone of voice over the years. It was just as clear that Clark still hadn't picked up on what it meant, or was just ignoring his wife. "What? What did I say? He's good-looking, a doctor, and right about her age. How is that not her type?"

Amy smiled. "You would be wasting Jim on me. I'm gay." Amy braced herself for the normal questions, but they didn't come.

"Well then, you should meet her other cousin, Heather."

Before Amy could answer, the family broke into discussion over whether or not Heather had broken up with her current girlfriend, and their thoughts on what that particular woman's intentions were. There seemed to be a mixed consensus. Matt walked over and whispered into Sarah's ear, and she handed him the car keys from her pocket. He kissed her cheek and walked to the other end of the table. Matt shook everyone's hand and kissed Sarah's mother good-bye.

Sarah obviously didn't want to talk about Matt having to leave, so she did what any friend would do in that situation. She threw Amy under the bus. "Amy can't meet Heather. She's dating someone."

Amy's ears were suddenly hot.

Before Matt shut the door behind him, he grinned at her. "Amy is *always* seeing someone."

Suddenly, the room was very quiet. There were a variety of answers she could give. Detailed explanations, excuses, a lot of things came to mind. The irony wasn't lost on her that this is exactly what she prepped clients for. Sure, there were usually cameras in front of them and microphones in every direction. But the waiting eyes of Sarah's family seemed just as intimidating.

Amy ran her finger around the top of her water glass and noted how the condensation was a variety of colors thanks to the Christmas lights that hung around the room. She also wondered if she was speeding up the melting process.

"Well, what's her name?" Clark would have made an excellent politician.

She thought it would be a perfect opportunity for a rescue, an assist from her friend, but it wasn't coming. Amy wasn't used to discussing anyone she was involved with. Their interactions usually didn't warrant disclosures. *Is Lena different?* "Lena. Lena Michaels." *Thanks, Sarah.* "Well," she said to Sarah, "remind me never to rob a bank with you."

Clark sat back in his chair. He rubbed his chin with the top of his hand. "Why does that name sound so familiar?"

His brother continued his thought for him. "Any relation to the Michaels murders that happened a few years back?"

Amy nodded. "Lena is their elder daughter." Amy's phone rang and she accidently said out loud, "Oh, thank God." Embarrassed, she excused herself before she looked down at her caller ID. It was a blocked number. "This is Amy."

"First, let me say I'm sorry. Second, you're welcome. Have a good holiday." It was Matt.

"Thank you, I'll be right there." She hung up the phone and walked back over to the table. "I'm so sorry. That was work. I'm going to have to go."

Sarah got up. "Do you need me?"

Amy shooed her away with a hand gesture. "No, no. I have this one. Enjoy the holiday with your family." She said thank you and good-bye to everyone, with the promise to return. Sarah walked her to the door.

Sarah hugged her. "Welcome to the family."

Amy laughed. "Thank you for everything."

Sarah leaned against the doorframe as Amy walked to her car. "That was Matt who called, wasn't it?"

Amy shrugged and got into her car. "Unlike you, I won't throw people under the bus." She grinned and waved as she drove away.

CHAPTER NINE

A my had never spent Christmas alone. She was always with family. It didn't make her particularly sad; it was just different. *Lonely.* She spoke briefly with her parents, who were in Australia and raving about the summer weather. Amy thought she should have made a drinking game out of the amount of times her mom said, "Flip-flops and shorts on Christmas." Addison had called, but again, it was a brief discussion. She couldn't tell Amy exactly where she was. The thought unnerved her, but she couldn't tell her that. Amy assumed it wasn't because she was in a top-secret location, but rather that she didn't want her to worry. Addison never really stopped treating her like she was that eight-year-old girl, playing dress-up in her sister's clothes when she thought she wasn't paying attention.

Amy spent most of the day clock-watching, thinking of the time she'd finally get to see Lena again. She finally decided to text her, and wished her a Merry Christmas. She was excessively pleased when she received almost an immediate response back, mirroring the sentiment. She finally decided to break up the day by going for a jog. The streets would be almost empty, and her closet didn't need to be reorganized…again.

The cold San Francisco air was invigorating. She could feel it in her chest, the slight burn of the brisk air combined with the heat her body was creating. She loved this feeling. She was also pleased that the streets were practically empty. Well, aside from the ignored population of homeless she noticed now more than she ever had before. Not out of annoyance or disgust, but rather concern and empathy. Seeing them at Lands End had changed her outlook on this demographic. She had spoken with several people while she was there and was truly surprised by how many of them were a product of horrible circumstances. Yes, there were a portion of them that suffered from mental illness, and those who were plagued with drug addiction, but they didn't make up the majority. She stopped when she saw a particular man huddled beneath a child's blanket. She recognized it as one she had passed out at Lands End, remembering she was impressed by the intricate embroidery. She opened her zipper pocket in her windbreaker and pulled out the twenty-dollar bill she carried when she ran, in case of an emergency. She handed it to him and he closed his hand over the top of hers.

"Merry Christmas." He held the note close to his heart and gave her a sad smile.

Amy started to move away, humbled that he could say the words, given his situation. She wasn't paying attention, and when she turned, she ran straight into a woman who was bent over, fixing her dog's collar. The woman stood up as Amy was in the middle of her profuse apology. Stunned, Amy fought to breathe properly. She had looked at that face thousands of times, the eyes dark brown with flecks of gold. They were the eyes that had filled with tears because of a sprained ankle after a mishap on a volleyball court. They were the eyes she had fallen asleep looking into, naming children they never had. "Evie?"

"Amy?"

Evie's arms, that at one time had given her comfort, a safe place, but were now unfamiliar, wrapped around her, but Amy couldn't move. She was stuck, frozen in disbelief, or rage. She didn't know which. Evie continued to hug her, and Amy managed to move her arms just enough to push her away.

Once she was at arm's length, she was finally able to speak. "What are you doing here, Evie?"

Evie seemed oddly surprised that Amy didn't return her warm welcome. Apparently, not much had changed. Evie was still unaware and self-centered. "I actually go by Evelyn now. I just started a new job. I got here a few weeks ago." She moved her dark hair out of her eyes. It had always been a nervous habit of hers, and Amy was caught off guard that she still recognized it as such.

Amy felt the anger surge through her. It started at the tips of her fingers and worked itself up all the way to her neck, a hot flush consuming her. It was probably anger. Anger mixed with betrayal and resentment, and probably a hundred other emotions she couldn't name. Evie, or Evelyn, whatever she was calling herself, was staring at her, probably waiting for a response.

"How have you been?"

Amy did the only thing she could think to do. She put her earphones back in, maneuvered around the ghost from Christmas past, and kept running.

By the time she got back to her apartment, she was trembling. She had run for a little over two hours, and her legs were weak. She grabbed a bottle of water out of the fridge, drank the entire thing, and then lay down on her floor. The couch would have been far too much effort. She stared at the ceiling, listening to the sound of her heart pound in her head. Faces flashed before her like movie scenes, the faces of the dozens of women since Evie. Some she could remember vividly, others were just a blur. She used them as a numbing ointment, possibly a crutch. A way to forget...or ignore...the gash that had been left on her heart by a woman who now apparently had a basset hound and lived in her city, probably close by. Christmas had definitely taken a turn she wasn't expecting.

❖

Lena hung up from her phone call and turned around to face the people watching her. "You guys should really get cable out here, if everyone is using my conversation with the manager as a source of entertainment."

Chloe got out of her seat and poured another cup of coffee. "You're going back tonight?"

Lena nodded. "I'm afraid we have to. My manager's wife and four-year-old both have the flu. There's no one to open the restaurant tomorrow."

Laura, surprisingly, seemed disappointed. Lena assumed it was because she had spent most of the day laughing and playing games with Ben.

Chloe noticed as well. "I can take her home with me on the twenty-seventh." She moved her head in Laura's direction. Lena crossed her arms, staring at her.

Laura's face lit up. "Can I please stay?"

Lena looked at her in disbelief. "You really want to stay?"

Her smile widened. "I really do."

Lena looked at Tina. "Is that okay with you?"

Tina put her arm around Laura. "Of course it is. You don't even have to ask."

Lena moved toward the room she was staying in. "Okay, it's all settled then."

Chloe followed right behind her. "Plus, it will give you some alone time with Amy."

Lena started putting her few things into her bag and rolled her eyes. "Hand me that shirt." She caught the shirt Chloe lobbed at her. "That's not why I am going back early."

Chloe smiled. "Oh, I know. Just a happy coincidence."

"I'm not even seeing her until tomorrow."

Chloe put Lena's gifts into one of the bags she had brought. "That's because you weren't originally going back *until* tomorrow. You're going back early now."

Lena walked out of the room and came back in with her toiletries. "Suddenly, you're Team Amy? Did I miss something?"

Chloe shrugged. "I want you to be happy, Lee. If she could possibly do that, then yes, I'm Team Amy." Chloe smiled. "But…"

Lena shook her head. "I knew there would be an asterisk."

"I will find a reason to sue the crap out of her if she even so much as bruises that ridiculously big heart of yours."

Lena finished putting everything in her bag and walked over to Chloe. She hugged her. "Thank you. Thank you for always being my best friend."

Chloe squeezed her and then pushed her away. "As if I had a choice. We were betrothed at birth."

Lena said good-bye to her sister and Chloe's family. Tina followed her out to her car and handed her a small box. "Tina, we're only supposed to exchange one present."

Tina nodded. "Just open it, honey." Lena pulled off the ribbon and opened the box. She recognized it immediately. Her mother had worn the mirror image of it every day of Lena's life. Lena pulled out the silver bracelet, feeling her eyes well up with tears. She closed her fingers around it and squeezed her eyes shut.

"I want you to have it."

Lena couldn't stop the tears that rolled down her cheeks. "I can't take this from you. You bought these bracelets together when you were eighteen years old."

Tina rubbed Lena's arms. "Take it, sweetheart. This one isn't mine. It was your mom's."

Lena couldn't help the quiet sob that escaped her throat. "I thought it was stolen in the robbery."

Tina explained. "So did I, until about three weeks after they passed. I was going through your mom's things and found a receipt from a jeweler. She had taken it in to get the clasp fixed. I went down there on the off chance she hadn't picked it up yet, and there it was. I've been holding on to it until the moment felt right. I hope that's okay."

Lena grabbed Tina and hugged her. "She loved this bracelet."

Tina rubbed Lena's back. "I know she did. I'm going to give mine to Chloe."

Lena pulled back to look at her. "Really?"

Tina was crying now. "Yes, really. We had always talked about giving them to you girls. I just couldn't bear to part with them until now."

Lena put it around her wrist, and Tina clasped it for her. "Thank you. Thank you so much."

Tina kissed her cheek. "You're so very welcome, honey."

Lena's heart was filled. Filled with gratitude, appreciation, and a bit of sadness. She stared at her mother's best friend, knowing she felt the same thing.

"You better get going. I don't want you driving in the dark on these mountain roads."

Lena kissed her cheek one last time. "I'll text you when I get back."

"Please do."

Lena started the car and drove away.

She watched the streetlights slowly fade away in the reflection of her rearview mirror, as she maneuvered up the mountain pass that was only illuminated by the headlights of those also venturing out this particular holiday evening. She glanced down at the bracelet wrapped around her wrist. Its presence should've made her long for her mother. It should've made her sad. It didn't. Lena felt like she had a piece of her mother's heart, right there with her. It seemed to tether her to her mother's plane of existence and to her own world. It was a symbol of friendship, love, and of the way life changes. She loved it.

The roads were empty. Not just beat-the-morning-commute kind of empty, but post-apocalyptic kind of empty. In contrast, Lena wasn't feeling empty at all. She was hopeful, excited, and could still feel the tingling of love and belonging that Tina had gifted her with. Laura staying behind gave her a sense of peace, and the anticipation of seeing Amy was pulsating through her body. This was the best Christmas she'd had in a very long time. She didn't time it, that would have been silly, but her smile carried her through most of the four-hour drive home.

❖

Amy stayed in the hot shower much longer than what was considered appropriate for the California drought, which had become a way of life over the last few years, regardless of the time of year. She felt guilty about it, but the hot water on her tired body felt magnificent. She walked out to her kitchen with her fluffy white robe tied tight around her waist. She opened the fridge and shut it again. Each time she'd opened it hoping for a different outcome, that some little food fairy would have magically filled it with something other than a moldy orange and out-of-date milk. She picked up her phone to call for Chinese takeout when it rang. Her heart sped up when she read Lena's name on the display.

"Hello?"

"Hi, Amy. Merry Christmas." There were butterflies in Amy's stomach. She hadn't thought her body was still capable of reacting to someone that way. She liked it. A lot.

"Hi, Lena. Merry Christmas."

There was a brief silence before Lena spoke again. "I, umm…I was wondering if you were busy tonight."

Amy began to pace. *What does that mean?* "No. I don't have anything planned." *That was an okay answer. Right?*

"Have you eaten?"

Amy put her hand to her stomach and felt it grumble. "No, not yet."

"Would you like to?"

Amy moved toward her bedroom, trying not to sound as eager as she felt. "Sure. Yes. I mean, I need to eat. You're going to have to eat. We should do that...together." She rolled her eyes at herself as she started to pull clothes from hangers. Lena went on.

"Okay, great. I don't really want to sit in a restaurant. I'll stop and grab something, if that's okay? We can either eat at my place or yours."

Amy removed the towel from her head and was trying to fasten her bra with one hand. "There's a really good Chinese place right down the street from me. If you don't mind stopping, we could get takeout from there."

"Sure. Sounds good. Why don't you call and order it, and I'll swing by and grab the food. Text me the address, as well as yours. There really isn't anything I don't like, so just get whatever."

Amy had on her unclasped bra, one sock, and was halfway through the process of getting her pants on. *Whoa, girl. Slow down.* "Okay. See you in a bit." Amy threw her phone onto her bed and looked in the mirror. *Shit.*

CHAPTER TEN

Lena looked at herself one last time in the reflection of her driver side window. She had decided to change out of the hoodie she had pulled over her shirt for the drive home. Now, she wore a charcoal V-neck sweater and faded jeans. She placed the food and bottle of wine on top of her car and ran her hands through her hair. *What am I doing?* She had spent the several hours it took to get back from Tahoe thinking about her life and the people in it. She was lucky to have the friends she did, and she loved her sister. Yes, she tried her patience and pushed her to the edge of a mental breakdown from time to time, but she did love her. Her thoughts kept shifting back to Amy. She had wanted to see her and called her on impulse. Now, as she looked at her reflection, she wasn't sure she had made the right choice. *What if Chloe is right? What if she's got ulterior motives?* Lena shook it off. She was nervous. She hadn't been on a date or interested in anyone in ages. *It's just jitters. I can do this. I totally can.* She grabbed the bags and headed into Amy's building.

The lobby was impressive, with white marble walls and pristine black tile. Lena walked over to the expansive wall that listed the apartment numbers without names and pushed the button that linked her to Amy's. At first, there was no answer.

Lena waited a few moments and pushed it again. Finally, a winded Amy answered.

"Sorry about that. Walk over to the elevator and push my apartment number again. I'll buzz you in."

"Fancy." Lena did as she was told. The buzzes came one after another. *Too late to turn back now.* The doors opened, and Lena walked down the hallway that was just as impressive as the lobby, until she found herself in front of Amy's door. She paused again before she knocked, cracking her neck and wishing her palms didn't feel sweaty.

Amy opened the door before she had a chance to turn around and run. "Hi."

Lena held up the Chinese food and bottle of wine. "I come bearing gifts."

Amy moved to the side to allow Lena in. "Great. Leave it on the counter and I'll see you tomorrow."

Lena laughed as she walked past her to the kitchen and placed the food on the counter. Amy already had plates and silverware out, but she walked to the cabinet to grab wine glasses. Lena watched her move. She was incredibly beautiful. Her dark hair was pulled back, and the red sweater she was wearing showed her neck and collarbone. She wore a thin gold necklace that lay perfectly in the gap. Amy put two wine glasses in her hand and grabbed a corkscrew from a drawer.

Lena busied herself with pulling the food out of the bag and placing it on the counter. "How was your Christmas?"

Amy cocked her head to the side. A strange look crossed her face. "It was…you know what…it got a whole lot better when you called."

That simple statement burned in Lena's chest. "Good. I'm glad I made your day better."

Amy poured the red wine and handed Lena a glass. "You really did." They dished up and sat down to eat.

Lena watched Amy move the food around on her plate. She needed to make conversation before her staring turned into creepy stalker leering. "So, what did you do yesterday?"

Amy took a bite of food. "I ended up going to Sarah's parents' house for dinner. It was kind of a last-minute thing, but I actually had a really good time. How about you?"

Lena finished chewing and took a sip of her wine. "We spend every Christmas up in Tahoe. Chloe's parents have a cabin there. Chloe's mom, Tina, and my mom were best friends since childhood."

Amy was staring at her contemplatively. "Is this the hardest time of year for you? So close to when your parents passed?"

Lena ate another bite of rice, thinking the question over. "No. I mean, it's never easy, but it does get a little more bearable every year. I have nothing but good memories of this time of year and being in Tahoe. Chloe's family is like my family, which makes me really lucky."

"I can't even begin to imagine what it must be like for you."

"I worry more about Laura than I do myself. She's practically grown up without parents. That's not ideal, obviously."

Amy put her hand on Lena's arm. There it was again. That feeling was there every time they touched. Lena had never experienced anything like it. She felt it through her whole body, not just where Amy's hand lay. It was incredible.

"She has you. It was the best possible outcome, considering the circumstances."

Lena forced herself to listen to the words that were coming from her mouth and ignore the way her body was reacting. "I'm not sure she would agree with you."

Amy didn't pull her hand away, and her grip got slightly tighter. She adjusted in her seat, bringing her body even closer to Lena. "She's a teenager. She doesn't really like anyone except her friends, and that's probably not always true either."

The tone in Amy's voice had changed. It had gotten quieter, a little deeper. Lena forced herself to swallow as Amy's mouth came up to her jaw. She brushed her lips against its corner and inched them down to her chin. "Can we stop talking about my sister now?"

Amy didn't respond with words. She moved so she straddled Lena's waist and sat down. Her toned arms came around Lena's neck, and Amy's perfectly green eyes stared into hers. "We don't have to talk about anything if you don't want to."

Lena didn't want to talk. She wasn't sure she could put a coherent sentence together if she needed to, at the moment. She watched as the corner of Amy's mouth quirked up in a half smile, as though she knew exactly what Lena was thinking. Lena slowly slid her hands up Amy's thighs until she reached her waist. Amy's cheeks flushed, and she watched her take a deep breath. Watching her was hypnotizing.

Lena leaned forward and kissed Amy's cheek. She slowly moved her way up her jaw, and Amy's arm tightened around Lena's neck, pulling her closer. Lena reached the bottom of her ear and lightly bit down. Amy moved her head down and kissed Lena with a fierceness that Lena had never experienced.

Buzz. Buzz.

Lena pulled her mouth away, needing a moment to breathe, and vaguely aware of the door buzzer going insistently. The sudden halt seemed to bring Amy back as well.

Amy stared at her door almost as though she was trying to see through it. It buzzed again. She kissed Lena quickly before getting up. "Don't move." Amy quickly went over to her door and pushed the buzzer in response. "Who is it?"

"Hey there. I knew you were going to be alone tonight. I brought some food. I thought maybe we could spend this Christmas like we did the last one. You know, naked in bed, eating dessert."

Amy looked back at Lena before she responded, her face bright red. "Hey, Britt, I have company, actually. Sorry."

"Oh, okay. Have you had a chance to talk to Lena for me?"

Amy shook her head and closed her eyes. "I have to go."

Lena had heard enough. She felt foolish. Chloe had been right. Amy was using her, though for what, she couldn't imagine. And clearly, she and Brittany were more than friends.

Amy stepped in front of her, her palms up in a pleading gesture. "It's not what it looks like."

"Really? What do you think it looks like?"

Amy took Lena's hands in her own. "Okay. You're either thinking I'm sleeping with Brittany, or we're in cahoots or something."

"Are you sleeping with her?"

"No, but I have."

"Did she ask you to talk to me about the interview?"

"Yes. She'd like to change the angle to be more about your parents and your sister. She really thinks it could help. Maybe the police would reopen the case. Nothing she didn't tell you herself, I swear."

Lena stared at a spot on the table. Emotions came at her from every angle, twisting her up inside. "When were you planning on telling me? After you slept with me? When it would have been easier to convince me?"

"No. It's not like that."

"Not like what, Amy? Not like you were trying to use me to help advance your friend's, or whatever she is to you, career?"

Amy stayed silent, and her face had gone pale. Her eyes showed her hurt, but Lena wasn't about to fall for it.

"Are you so used to spinning a story you don't even realize when you're doing it?"

"Lena, please. Hear me out."

"I have to go."

Lena walked out and leaned against the wall in the elevator. She was angry, hurt, and confused. The thought that Amy was trying to deceive her in any way made her ill. When she got outside, Brittany pulled up beside her on her motorcycle. Lena was sure she probably looked out of sorts, and the last person in the world she wanted to see, aside from Amy, was the person Amy had been sleeping with.

"Hey."

Lena crossed her arms in an attempt to keep warm. "Hey." Brittany looked ridiculously cool in her leather jacket and pants. *At least I understand why Amy...and how could I think she was interested in me, compared to that?*

Brittany pointed up in the direction of Amy's apartment. "I'm sorry if I interrupted anything."

Lena put her hand up. "It's fine. You probably interrupted just in the nick of time."

She inclined her head as though accepting the answer. Clearly, the woman was too cool to ask any prying questions. *She gets other people to do it for her.*

"Are we still on for tomorrow?"

Lena didn't know if she was angry or impressed by this woman's brazen audacity. "Are you sure you just don't want Amy to do the interview for you?"

Brittany seemed confused by the question. "Amy? No, I had just asked her to talk to you, because you two seemed close and I didn't want to step on your toes."

Lena put her hands on her hips. "You don't seem to have a problem overstepping your bounds to me."

"Lena, I don't know what you're talking about."

Lena took a step closer and pointed up at Amy's window. "If you have a question for me, ask me. Don't get your girlfriend, or whatever she is, to do it for you."

Brittany huffed. "Amy isn't my girlfriend. She never has been."

Lena waited for a further explanation, but Brittany gave no indication she was going to give one. She needed to get out of here. She turned to walk toward the parking garage. "I said I would do this interview and I will. Be at Lands End at eight in the morning."

Brittany put her helmet on and flipped up the front portion, revealing her eyes and mouth. "I would be there at three in the morning if that's what you wanted. See you tomorrow."

The bike took off down the near empty street with a roar. Lena rolled her eyes and shoved her hands in her pockets. She got in her car and drove away, berating herself for not listening to her instincts. *I knew she was trouble, and I let myself hope anyway. Stupid.*

Amy watched the two women from the security of her balcony. She could practically feel Lena's rage, even from so far away. She leaned against her railing, watching the red wine swirl around with each flick of her wrist. She brought it up to her mouth and finished the rest with one gulp. Then she plopped down on her lounge chair. *Worst Christmas ever.* The day had started with so much promise. Then Evie. *Evelyn.* Her first reaction was to blame her for everything that transpired after. S*he's the reason I slept with all those women. The reason I keep everyone at a distance.* Amy even went as far as to blame her for Brittany showing up tonight. But that wasn't reality. Amy made the choices she made; they were hers to own. Every day at work, she saw people who blamed others for their mistakes, and she helped them believe it. She wouldn't allow herself to be one of those people. Yes, Evelyn was the reason her heart was broken; she was the reason she had dropped twenty pounds following that horrible morning in college. But everything since then had been Amy's choice. She shut herself off in order to avoid pain, and in doing so, she had closed herself off to all the good things that come with intimacy, too. *Shit. It was easier when it was just her fault.*

Then there was Lena. *That went sideways in record time.* This was usually the moment where Amy would write a woman off for good. Too much complication, too much hassle, and too many emotions. But that was before. Before someone had made her laugh, made her body light up and refused to leave her thoughts. Lena had caught a glimpse of something she didn't like, and they were going to need to talk about it. And, unlike her previous responses to emotional confrontations, she wanted to talk. She wanted to make Lena understand. The thought of Lena being upset with her, that she might be thinking she was untrustworthy, gave her a feeling of dread and made her feel sick to her stomach. *I have to fix this. Somehow.*

CHAPTER ELEVEN

Amy didn't know the actual time someone needed to physically be at a restaurant in order to open it. She figured seven in the morning was a safe bet. She sat in her car watching the way the sky changed as the sun rose, and morning light glistened off the Pacific Ocean. This morning, this day, felt different from others. She felt a sense of peace and calm for the first time in years. Her normal, jaded demeanor felt slightly sanded down, diluted. She was usually in the office by this time, two hours prior to everyone else. She had never been late for work, but this morning that didn't seem important. She needed to talk to Lena.

Amy caught a glimpse in her rearview mirror of a light green Prius as it pulled into the parking lot. Her heart sped up, partially out of nervousness and partially because that was the effect Lena had on her. Amy got out of her car and waited for Lena at the front door. Lena looked her up and down for a moment, and although Amy was hoping to see the smile she loved, she clearly wasn't going to be rewarded with that yet.

Lena sipped her coffee from a mug that had pictures of her and her sister wrapped around it. "I forgot what you looked like dressed for work."

Amy looked down at her suit, suddenly self-conscious. She ran her hands over her stomach, an old nervous habit she'd long tried to break. But then, she couldn't remember ever being this nervous. "I wanted to talk to you before either of us started our day."

Lena turned to unlock the doors. "You could have called."

Amy followed closely behind. Calling hadn't been an option. She knew the importance of face-to-face conversations. "I wanted to actually see you. I wanted to apologize in person."

Lena opened the door and waited for Amy to follow her in. Once Amy was in, Lena entered a series of numbers on an electric keypad and then locked the door again. "I actually wanted to talk to you, too. You start."

She wanted to talk to me. That's good, right? She continued to follow Lena through the main dining area and toward her office, turning on lights as she moved through the building. "I should have told you about Brittany."

Once they were in her office, Lena finally faced her. "Which part about Brittany?"

Amy took a step closer, wanting to see if Lena moved away, but she didn't. "All of it. I should have told you. Not because I think we have to disclose all our history as quickly as possible, but because you had asked. I intentionally left out certain parts, and I shouldn't have. Old habits, I suppose. I'm sorry."

Lena nodded and sighed softly. "We weren't together. You don't owe me anything."

Amy desperately wanted to touch her, but her body language suggested it wouldn't be welcome yet. "I should have been more honest. I'm not used to disclosing things about myself or my history. I'm not really good at doing anything except casual. Like you said, maybe I even use spin on my own life, I'm so used to doing it in my work life. I hadn't thought of it that way, really. It will take a little time to get used to doing things differently."

Lena's expression was deadly serious, her gaze searching. There was heat in her eyes, but whether from anger or passion, Amy couldn't tell.

"Do you want to do things differently?"

Amy had flashes of Evie rush through her mind. "I wasn't always like this, believe it or not."

Lena's intent gaze suggested she continue.

"My college girlfriend, Evie. We'd been together for three years and were making plans for the future. I really believed we were going to spend our lives together." Amy felt her voice start to trail off, and a lump formed in the back of her throat. She took a moment to clear it. "Anyway, she decided she wanted to end things. There was no real explanation, no warning. She was actually only going to leave a note. A few sentences. She thought a few years could be swept away by saying that we needed to grow, become who we were meant to, and we could only do that apart. I mean, it was clearly bullshit. That was Evie though. She had a way of minimizing everything. We had an epic fight, said a lot of things to one another we shouldn't have. I happened to come home right before she left." Amy wiped away a tear she hadn't realized until then had started its way down her cheek. "Since then, I haven't allowed myself to get close to anyone. Actually, I haven't really wanted to get close to anyone."

Lena's expression had softened. "And now it's different?"

"*You* are different. I don't want to do things the way I have been, not this time."

Amy leaned forward and kissed her. It was a soft, slow kiss intended to tell Lena she did want to do things differently.

Amy's phone began to ring in her pocket, and a soft noise of disappointment came out of Lena's throat. Amy pulled out the phone and looked at the caller ID. She gave Lena an apologetic look and pushed the IGNORE button. "I need to go into the office."

Lena took both her hands. "I understand. I can only imagine what the wealthy people of San Francisco managed to get themselves into over Christmas."

Amy kissed her again. "Can I still see you tonight? I should be off around seven."

Lena nodded. "I'd like that. But we still need to talk things through, okay?"

Amy wouldn't have been able to hide her smile if she had wanted to, but she didn't. She didn't want to hide anything, anymore. "I understand. Pick you up from your place at eight?

"Sounds good."

Amy kissed her again. "Great. See you then." She forced herself not to skip out of the office. It wasn't until she got to the front door that she realized she needed to be let out. She turned around to find an amused Lena a few steps behind.

"I need to unlock the door for you."

Amy felt her cheeks flush. "Yeah. I just realized that."

Lena leaned around her, putting the key back into the door. The sensation of their arms brushing against each other was almost overwhelming. Amy didn't want to go anywhere. She couldn't remember when she had ever felt like that, when something personal made her want to put her work aside.

"Amy, wait."

Amy turned around, hoping there would be more kissing.

"Stay for the interview. I mean, I haven't talked about this publically before. I haven't talked about what happened." Lena took a step closer to her. "I guess I would feel better if someone was here, you know, with me."

Amy answered without regard to work, without worrying about the consequences. "Of course."

They walked back into the restaurant and toward Lena's office. Once inside, Lena motioned to her desk. "You can use my computer to answer any emails or do whatever you need to do. I've got things to do before Brittany gets here."

Amy sat down and pulled out her tablet. "Thank you. I have everything that I need right here."

Lena walked toward the door. "I'll be in the kitchen if there's anything you need. And, Amy, thank you for staying."

Amy smiled up at her. "Thank you for asking."

❖

The staff started to arrive, prepping the kitchen and the dining area for the customers that would be outside their door in a few hours. Lena moved around the dining area, correcting tablecloths to their exact position and checking silverware. A staff member walked up and told her someone was at the front door for her. Lena took a deep breath and walked to the front of the restaurant.

Lena was starting to think that Brittany only owned clothes that could double for motorcycle wear. Brittany had a way about her, a confident swagger. She was confident, cool, and her hair never seemed to be out of place, even after she'd worn a helmet. Lena walked with her to her office. "I asked Amy to sit in on the interview." Brittany nodded her acceptance, seemingly unfazed by the information.

Once inside, Amy got up and moved to the corner of the room, letting Lena take her seat behind the desk. Brittany shot her a half smile and took her seat as well. "Thank you for agreeing to do this. I know it wasn't something you really wanted to do. If it's okay with you, I'm going to record this, but if there's something you specifically don't want on the record, let me know."

Lena nodded. She appreciated that Brittany was going to make that allowance. In her experience, most reporters were interested in the story and weren't all that worried about their subject's concerns. "Thank you for that. Also, before we get started, I wanted to apologize for last night. I overreacted." She shot a glance at Amy, who seemed to be intently listening to the exchange. Amy's encouraging smile helped settle her nerves.

Brittany held up her hand. "It's okay. I can only imagine what the situation looked like. And you were right. I should've talked to you and not Amy. That was my bad."

Lena was going to explain further, but it didn't seem necessary. Brittany seemed genuine, but Lena was fighting back the impulse to like her, at least until she knew more about her intentions.

Brittany pulled out a notebook and a pen. "Why don't we start by you telling me what you want me to know about your parents?"

Lena leaned back in her chair. She hadn't actually thought about what this interview would entail. She tried to focus, and pulled on cherished memories. "They were amazing people. I'm sure most people say that about their parents, but mine really were. My mom was kind, smart, and selfless. She spent almost all of her free time volunteering, working with the homeless. My dad was a bit of a goof. He liked to play practical jokes and tell stories you knew were exaggerated, but you wanted to hear anyway because of the way he told them. They met and married at nineteen. My mom was working here, at Lands End, for the previous owner. She started out by serving at sixteen and then worked her way up. Being a chef was the only thing she had ever wanted to do, but culinary school is expensive. My grandmother had passed away when my mom was very young, and then my grandfather passed when she was seventeen. The owner took my mom under her wing. She never had any formal training, but she was the best. Anyway, my dad went to school here and worked as a delivery driver. He asked her out fourteen times before she finally said yes. A year later, they were married."

Brittany looked up from her notes. "What about your dad's parents?"

Lena shook her head. "None. I mean, he obviously had them, but they were never part of our lives. There was a falling out of some sort before he left for college. I tried to find them when my parents passed, but I couldn't. Not because I wanted them to take Laura, but because I thought they would want to know. I believe my dad has a brother, too." Lena could tell Brittany's mind was turning. She forced herself not to look at Amy. She was aware of her presence. She could feel it in every part of her body, but she was worried looking up at Amy would make her cry as she delved into old memories.

"Do you want to find them?"

"No."

"You don't think it's lonely? Without any other family?"

"I have family. I have my sister, and my best friend Chloe's family. They treat us like their own. That's enough for us."

"Does your sister agree?"

"Is that really pertinent to your story?" Brittany was quiet for a moment. Lena thought she would push more but she didn't.

"Okay, I'm sorry. Please continue."

"They were married in 1979. My dad finished business school, and my mom kept working here. They purchased a house when a family could still afford a home in San Francisco for a reasonable price. They tried for years to have kids and finally got pregnant with me. When I was about two, Dorothy, the woman that owned Lands End, passed away and left it to my mom. My mom was the only family she really had. Eleven years later, my sister was born. I went off to college when she was seven. I was attending UC Davis, to be a social worker."

"What happened that night?"

Lena turned to look at the picture of her parents that she had hanging on her wall. There were several pictures of them throughout the restaurant as well, but this was her favorite. It was a moment they didn't know their picture was being taken. Tina had taken it at a picnic they were having in Golden Gate Park. They were young, in love, and they were perfect. "It was October twenty-third. I got a call from the hospital. There had been a robbery. Everyone had been shot and I needed to come down right away." Lena hadn't told anyone about this night in years. She had thought about it, yes. But she hadn't retold it out loud. She focused on continuing to hold back tears. "The news about Laura came first. She was going to make it. She had lost a lot of blood, but she was going to be okay. It's silly when they use the term 'make it.' I mean, yes, she was going to survive. But 'make it'? What does that mean?"

Brittany shook her head. "I don't know."

"My parents, however, did not. That was is it. There was nothing else. They didn't 'make it.' Eight hours before, they were happy, healthy, vibrant people, and then they were just gone." Lena wiped a tear off her cheek, frustrated she couldn't keep her emotions in check. "I took Laura home a few days later. I quit school and took over Lands End. My sister gave a pretty detailed description of what happened, and they had a few leads, but they never panned out to anything. They never caught him."

Brittany was quiet for what seemed like ages, though it was probably only a moment. "The dinner you serve on the twenty-third of every month, is that for you, or for your parents?"

Lena took a sip of water. "Both. It was so painful. What happened almost consumed me, so I wanted to do something that celebrated them and brought me some peace. That dinner is what I came up with. My parents loved this city. They both, but especially my mom, devoted so much time to the homeless, it seemed like the most obvious answer. It helps me believe she still lives on, here, with them and the restaurant."

"That empty table you keep in the dining area, the one that's always set, is that for them?"

"Yes." Lena was surprised at the emotion that showed on Brittany's face. She was writing, but her face was flushed.

"What would you change? Not the obvious, to still have your parents here. What would you have done differently?"

Lena had honestly never thought about it. For so long, she struggled just to make it from one day to the next. Always worried about if she was messing things up for Laura, if she was making the right choices with Lands End. "I would have made more time for myself." She briefly froze when the words left her mouth. "God, that's selfish."

"What do you hope is your family's legacy?"

"I guess the obvious answer is Lands End, but I hope that isn't all we're known for. I would like my parents' legacy to be what we try to do for the community. I would like to think we made a difference."

"Is there anything you want people to know about you and Laura that you think everyone has gotten wrong?"

Lena didn't need to think long about this answer. She had thought it a thousand times, every time she'd picked up a newspaper about what had happened. "We're more than 'those poor little girls who lost their parents.' I'm not saying it's been easy. There were days, weeks, even months, where it seemed unbearable and I wasn't sure if we would make it. But we have and we're more than a tag line of a tragedy filed under the unsolved cases of San Francisco."

Brittany grinned, nodding. "Would you mind if I talked to your sister?"

Lena's immediate response was to say that she did mind, that she didn't want her sister to have to live through this again. But she didn't know if it was her decision to make. Regardless of her desire to protect Laura, this was something she needed to decide, on her own. She wasn't a child to be protected anymore. If the past few months had taught her anything, it was that Laura was growing up. "You can ask her. If she says no, that's it though." Brittany nodded. "She'll be back tomorrow afternoon. She's scheduled to work here the morning after. You can come by then and ask her."

Brittany stopped recording and put her things away in her bag. She stood and Lena shook Brittany's hand. "Thank you so much, Lena."

Lena nodded. Brittany walked out of the room without talking to Amy, but they acknowledged each other, with Amy giving Brittany a half smile.

Lena leaned against her desk. The interview had been far more draining than she had anticipated. Amy took her hand. "Thank you for letting me be here, for letting me in."

Lena's eyes were burning. Fighting the tears had aggravated them. "Thank you for staying."

"I'm so glad I did." She squeezed Lena's fingers. "Everything you two have been through, overcome, it's inspiring."

"Laura is the strong one. She lived through the worst part."

Amy hugged her. The sudden closeness was surprising and welcomed. Amy whispered, "She couldn't have done it without you."

Lena felt Amy's phone vibrate against her. "You should get to work. I know you're late."

Amy kissed her cheek. "It's nothing that couldn't wait."

"Thank you again for staying. It really means a lot to me."

Amy kissed her cheek again. "See you tonight?"

Lena nodded. "Yes, I'd really like that."

Amy walked toward the door, turning back one last time to smile at Lena, and even as exhausted as she was, Lena's stomach still flipped at the way that smile made her feel.

Amy checked her watch for the fiftieth time that day. Waiting to see Lena again was like waiting for a giant present you knew you were getting. *What's happening to me?* She thought back on the events from earlier that morning. She had never known someone like Lena Michaels. The strength that lived inside her was unlike anything she'd ever witnessed. Amy felt invigorated by being around her, by knowing Lena had thought her worthy to let her in. She felt trusted and appreciated. It was intoxicating.

She had fielded the phone calls from the partners who were still out of the office pertaining to the new clients they wanted a meeting with, "as soon as humanly possible." Getting a meeting with anyone this time of year wasn't the easiest of tasks. Especially, when you were talking about one of the fastest growing companies in not only the Bay Area, but the world. They believed in family time and vacation hours at the holidays. But Amy had worked her magic, and they had a meeting with Uber Technologies the following week.

She was doing a small victory spin in her chair when Sarah knocked on her already open door.

"Feeling pretty good about yourself, I see."

Amy pretended her fingers were guns, blew on them, and then stuck them into her pockets.

"Don't do that again. You look absurd."

Amy laughed. "You're no fun."

Sarah dropped a set of files on her desk. "And you're having too much fun."

Amy saw the name on top—Peter Reynolds. She didn't open it. She didn't want to. "What is that? Please tell me he wasn't with any underage girls."

Sarah sighed. "No, not since the last incident." She pointed. "Those are tweets from his wife. They're pretty passive aggressive, and she seems to be at her boiling point. If you want to keep this under wraps, she's going to need dealing with."

"When is their next game?"

Sarah scrolled through her tablet. "They have their last divisional game New Year's weekend. But they made the playoffs, so their season could potentially last another month."

"Is the game home or away?"

"Arizona."

"Good. That means they'll be out of town most of the week. Hopefully, distance makes the heart grow fonder." She paused. "But just in case, see if you can get me a meeting with her tomorrow morning."

"Do you want me to send one of the associates?"

"No. I'll take care of it."

Sarah made a few notes in her tablet. "Where are you taking her tonight?"

"I was thinking of that new Asia Bistro that opened downtown."

Sarah shook her head in disapproval. Amy didn't understand what she had done wrong. "What?"

Sarah perched on the edge of Amy's desk. "She owns a restaurant. You can't take her to another for a first date."

"Is this our first date? It's really hard to tell. I feel like we've had several."

"Yes, it is your first real outing together. For someone so unbelievably smart, you sure are dumb sometimes."

Amy tapped her pen against her chin and turned back around to look out her window. "It should be special then."

"Yes. It should be. If you want her to think of you as special, you have to show her." Sarah stood and started toward the door. "I'm leaving at five tonight. If you need anything, now is the time to tell me.

Amy was lost in thought. "No. Have a good night."

Chapter Twelve

Lena had no idea what Amy had planned. She'd gotten a text that said to dress comfortably and warm. She didn't know if they were going downtown, to the beach, or somewhere to hide a body. It had been a long day. But waiting to meet Amy, she felt alive, excited, giddy. She had gone back and forth about the beanie more times than she wanted to admit, and finally decided against it. Being cold was worth being sexy.

At two minutes after eight, the knock she had been waiting for all day finally sounded, and her pulse raced. She grabbed the coat off the hanger and opened the door.

Amy was standing there looking fantastic with her perfect smile and flushed cheeks. "Ready?"

"Absolutely." She shut the door and walked down to Amy's car, pushing aside the desire to pull her into the house and do entirely different things. She got in the passenger seat "Where are we going?"

Amy backed up the car without saying anything, and once she was positioned correctly on the road, she answered with a grin, "It's a surprise."

Amy held Lena's hand like it was the most natural thing in the world. Once again, the simple gesture both excited Lena and warmed her chest.

Amy looked over at her. "I know you've lived here your whole life, but one of my favorite things about this city is there are areas, hidden within other places, buried inside treasures. San Francisco is like a real life nesting doll."

Lena had never heard her city summed up so perfectly. Amy was right. A block meant the difference between Union Square, one of the most visited tourist attractions in the whole city, and the Tenderloin, a haven for drugs. Another area housed hipsters on one block, gangs on the next. The vast contrast was never ending.

Lena thought she knew every part of her beloved city. The hours she had spent wandering as a child and adult had afforded her countless treasures tourists never bothered to acquaint themselves with. As Amy made her last few turns, Lena felt her ears start to warm with excitement, and she didn't recognize anything. She looked around, soaking it in. There weren't many places that allowed you to see the stars that hung above a lit city, especially a city that was usually draped in fog, but this was an exception. Lena looked over at Amy waiting for an explanation.

Amy had a knowing grin on her face. "Please tell me I actually found a spot you have never been."

They both got out of the car. Amy walked around to the trunk and Lena said, "You have, and I'm impressed. My question is, how did you know it existed?"

Amy shrugged. "I remembered seeing a telescope in your living room when I was at your house. So I made a few phone calls and managed to get access to this piece of property. It's owned by one of my clients, and it's actually the second best place to look at stars. I figured you had no interest in going to the first, since it's at—"

Lena interrupted. "Lands End." No one had ever done anything like that for Lena before. Noticed something so subtle and went out of her way to make it special. "Thank you, Amy."

Amy grabbed the blanket, thermos of hot chocolate, and some camping mugs out of her trunk. "Oh, don't thank me yet. I have no idea how cold it's going to get up here. You might be begging me to take you home in a few minutes."

She laid out the blanket and poured the hot chocolate. They snuggled together on the blanket and stared at the city.

Lena held her cup tightly, the warmth welcome. "It really is beautiful." Lena spoke to Amy, but she was staring out at the seemingly endless ocean of city lights far below them. "You get so caught up in the day-to-day, I think you forget to sometimes take a step back and see all of this for what it really is."

"What is it?

Lena looked at Amy and smiled. "It's beautiful. It's beautiful in its chaos, in its daily transformation, in its uniqueness and its normality, all at the same time."

Amy took a sip of her hot chocolate. "I don't think I've ever known anyone like you, Lena Michaels."

Lena knew it was a compliment and she didn't take compliments well, so she changed the subject. "How was your day?"

"It was good. Thank you again for letting me be there for the interview this morning. Thank you for trusting me."

Lena took Amy's hand. She brought it up to her lips and ran them across her knuckles. "Thank you for being there for me. I didn't really know how I'd feel talking about everything, and it made it easier to have you there. And I appreciate you opening up to me about your past. That couldn't have been easy for you."

"It wasn't. Not because I miss her, I'm just not used to talking to people about it, about myself, and I'm not sure how to go about it. I should've told you about Brittany, though. There have been more than just Brittany, quite a few more, actually."

"I kind of gathered that."

"I don't do things like this." She pointed between herself and Lena. "I don't go on dates."

Lena waited for her to continue.

"But I would like to try. With you. I would like to try."

Lena leaned over, bringing her lips up to Amy's. She could feel Amy's breath against her mouth. The heat coming off her was intoxicating, and Lena wanted to be closer. But with the emotions of the last several days, she also didn't want to get caught up in something she couldn't control. "Let's just take it slow. Is that okay with you?"

Amy didn't respond; she only nodded.

"We can do a lot of this, though." She kissed Amy. It was slow, soft, and perfect. Amy's hand came up to Lena's face. Amy's touch, whether she knew it or not, was filled with reassurance and caring. It was tender and intimate. The touch itself made no noise, but it was as if a cannon went off inside Lena. She leaned into Amy's hand.

"Are you sure you're okay with taking things slow?" Lena was worried she wouldn't be at Amy's speed, especially given her sexual history. But she wanted this to be right, for both of their sakes.

"I want to do whatever you're comfortable with. This whole thing is new to me. I'll try to move at whatever speed you want."

Lena leaned over and kissed Amy again. "Let me be perfectly clear. I don't want this to come to a screeching halt. I just want us to get to know each other a little better before we jump into bed."

The grin on Amy's face looked mischievous. "What's your favorite color?"

Lena grinned back and pressed closer to her. "Blue."

"What's your favorite food?" Amy moved even closer.

"Anything Italian."

"Favorite candy?" Amy pushed the few strands of hair that had landed in Lena's eyes behind her ear.

"Milky Way."

"Really? That's unexpected." She kissed Lena. "I had you pegged as more of a Snickers kind of girl."

Lena kissed her back, smiling against Amy's mouth. "I see what you're doing."

"I'm getting to know you a little bit." Amy slowly ran her hand up Lena's leg.

"Is that what you call it?" Lena didn't stop her hand, she didn't want to. She also wanted to see what Amy's idea of slow was.

Amy's hand stopped moving up her leg, but she kept her closeness the same, and Lena was reveling in it.

"Did you have any pets?"

Lena started laughing. "Man, you're really working for this."

Amy shrugged. "I go after what I want."

"Have you ever *not* gotten what you wanted?"

Amy thought about it for a moment. "Not in a very long time."

Lena thought Amy was referencing the woman from college again. She didn't want her thinking about that at all, or ever again, if she could help it. "Lie back."

Amy wiggled her eyebrows. "I like your idea of slow."

Lena pushed her backward. "Just lie down."

Lena lay down next to her and took her hand. She pointed up at the sky. "See Orion's Belt? If you look a little above that you can see the horns and chest of Taurus." Lena continued to point. She could feel Amy's attention moving to follow her hand. "Zeus fell in love with a princess named Europa. Like, completely obsessed with her. So he transformed himself into a bull in order not to scare her or the maidens. Obviously, he had to be a pretty friendly bull. Anyway, he convinced her to sit on his back while he took a walk in the ocean. He started paddling out to sea, and eventually they landed on Crete, where he told her who he really was. Then he seduced her and they had three sons."

Amy looked over at her. "I thought Zeus was married."

"He was, six times actually, but that never stopped him from having a multitude of sexual conquests. This was just one of many."

"Am I supposed to be Zeus, Taurus, or the princess?"

Lena laughed. "Well, Zeus and Taurus are technically the same, and you aren't supposed to be any of them."

"I don't want to be Zeus...or that silly princess, for that matter."

"Just be Amy. I like Amy."

They lay together in silence for a little before Amy whispered, "Can I tell you something?"

Lena looked over. "Of course."

"I'm absolutely freezing. Can we get out of here?"

Lena sat up laughing. "Yes, let's go. Do you want to come back to my place and watch a movie?"

"Yes, please."

❖

In any other situation, Amy would be planning her exit strategy. But being around Lena was incredible. She made Amy feel like she could be anything, do anything, while at the same time it was okay to be exactly who she was. Amy had never felt like that with anyone. She pulled into Lena's driveway. "I know you said this morning that your sister is due back soon, but when is she actually coming home?"

"Chloe is bringing her back tomorrow. She wanted to stay up in Tahoe." She opened the car door and started up to the porch. "I assume because she wanted to spend more time with Ben, Chloe's little brother."

Amy was relieved for two reasons. One, Laura was interested in someone she assumed was closer to her age, seeing as Lena didn't seem to have a real issue with it. Two, because it would mean she would stay clear of Peter Reynolds, which was good for her as well. She continued to follow Lena up to the house. "How do you feel about that? Ben and Laura?"

Lena opened the door and walked in. "I'm not sure anything will come of it. But he's a much better decision than that scumbag you keep an eye on." Lena seemed to slow, probably replaying what she had just said.

"It's okay. What he did was terrible. I don't blame you for feeling like that about him."

They went inside and Lena started turning on lights. "How can you do it? Protect him the way you do."

Amy hung her jacket over the chair. She crossed her arms and thought about her answer. She had been asked the same question dozens of times. This time her answer had a different significance. It would shape what Lena thought of her, and that mattered deeply. "I would be lying if I said it was always easy. It's not. Some of the things these people do are shameful. I do my best to compartmentalize, keep myself separated from it. Not all public relations work is getting people out of trouble. But that's where the money is, and that's where my firm focuses."

Lena was listening, but Amy could tell her answer wasn't the one she was hoping for.

"Have you ever considered working somewhere else?"

"Honestly, I've always been so focused on making partner I've never considered leaving. This situation with Peter Reynolds, it's not what I typically spend my day doing. What happened with your sister and those other girls was ridiculous. I hope you know I don't condone what he was doing."

Lena nodded. "I know. I mean, I hope you wouldn't. It's just hard for me to imagine you being on his side."

"I'm not on his side. I'm just doing my job."

"What exactly is your job? I mean, you say you don't spend your days doing this type of thing, so what do you spend your days doing?"

Amy thought about it before she answered. She had given a scripted answer dozens of times before, to her parents, to friends, to women. Giving Lena an answer seemed to carry more weight than it had in those other instances. "Not all of our clients are trying to hide something. Some are just trying to deal with an off-the-cuff comment taken out of context, or trying to change their image after a bad business deal or divorce. Others are planning to run for public office and need to start a conversation in the media before someone else beats them to the punch."

Lena looked thoughtful, but still unsure. It made Amy consider the truth of what she was saying. "I used to think I was going to make a difference. I thought PR gave you the opportunity to bring a voice to organizations that didn't always have one, or that were overlooked. I mean, I knew there was a certain amount of 'spin' that would be required; it pays the bills after all. I just never thought it would take up so much of my time." She shrugged. "I guess I'm good at making bad situations go away and helping people put a better face on things. So the partners make use of that skill. But my real passion is helping organizations rebrand or rebuild to make themselves stronger. Giving second chances."

"I understand, I think." Lena walked around to the other side of her couch and motioned for Amy to come sit with her. "Let's watch a movie."

Amy wasn't sure if she had given Lena the answer she wanted, or the one she was hoping for, but it was the truth. The fact that Lena seemed to still want to be near her was a good sign. *She hasn't run away or thrown me out, cursing the gods for damning her.* Okay, that was a bit dramatic, but Amy couldn't seem to help herself. The comfort that Lena's hand on her leg brought her wasn't something she wanted to go away.

CHAPTER THIRTEEN

A my slowly opened her eyes. She was warm and surprisingly comfortable. She had fallen asleep with Lena on her couch, or more accurately, wedged on top of Lena, and pressed against the back of her couch. She pushed herself up and received a quiet moan from Lena, who looked beautiful even asleep with her hair mussed. She rubbed her eyes, wondering when was the last time she had actually slept with a woman, really slept. *Not since Evie...Evelyn. Whatever.*

Amy went into the bathroom. She found some mouthwash under the sink and did a thorough rinse. She looked at her phone and saw that it was four in the morning. It was no wonder she was up. This was the time she would normally go jogging. She needed to go home to shower and change for the day. That's what she *needed* to do. What she wanted to do was crawl back on top of Lena and stay there, for as long as she would let her.

She walked out of the bathroom and into the kitchen. She quietly got the coffee pot ready and set it to begin brewing at five. Then she cut up several pieces of fruit and left them in the fridge, along with a note. She walked back over and took a moment to watch Lena sleep. She gently pulled the blanket over her, and her heart skipped slightly when Lena murmured and curled into it. She leaned over, kissed her forehead, and quietly left.

❖

The smell of coffee brought Lena out of a deep sleep. She opened her eyes and looked over the top of the couch, expecting to find Amy. The disappointment stung more than she anticipated. She walked over and poured the cup of coffee, opened the fridge for the cream, and found a plate of fruit with a note.

I never had that much fun in Greek mythology class. Thank you. Sorry I couldn't stay, but I needed to get ready for work. I can't wait to see you again.—Amy

Lena pulled the fruit out of the fridge and read the note over and over while she sipped her coffee and devoured the strawberries and oranges. She realized they hadn't actually made plans to see each other again. That fact made her irrationally anxious. She grabbed her phone from the table. She clicked on the message icon next to Amy's name. *Thank you for breakfast. I hope you have a good day.* She hit delete. *Thank you for breakfast. I hope to see you soon.* Delete again. *Thank you for breakfast. I'll be your teacher any day.* She stared at the plethora of emoji choices. She hated emojis. She hit send; no little yellow smiley face was needed.

She continued to munch on the fruit, thinking back on the night before. Her chest warmed, and she smiled. Listening to Amy talk about her job, the way she explained it, made sense. Taking on cases like Peter Reynolds's wasn't her life's ambition, but it was something she needed to do in her line of work. Amy had made it clear she would rather be working on something with a little more substance, and that knowledge alone quieted some initial apprehensions that Lena had harbored.

She finished her breakfast and skipped up the stairs, humming a Britney Spears song she hadn't actually thought about in years. She didn't bother stopping herself. She didn't care if it was silly; she felt better than she had in a very long time.

❖

Amy drove up to Presidio Heights. She had joked with Sarah before she left that morning that even sneezing in this area of San Francisco would cost you a thousand dollars. A two-bedroom, two-bathroom home in this little nook of the city cost a million dollars. But if you were the type of person who needed fourteen bedrooms and some obscene number of bathrooms, there were options for you as well, as long as you were willing to spend eighteen million to live in this little eight-by-five block radius. It also happened to be where Peter Reynolds lived with his wife.

Amy parked and checked her phone. She had been texting with Lena all morning, and it made her a little bit sad to have to silence her phone in order to deal with this situation. Lena was funny, sweet, smart, and morally completely out of Amy's league. Amy had already decided not to point that last part out to her, on the off chance Lena wasn't aware.

It was raining that morning, a weather anomaly the entire state of California desperately needed. Years of below average rainfall and an almost non-existent snowpack had left the state in a perpetual state of drought, even in the winter. Amy cursed herself for not grabbing an umbrella. *Do I even own an umbrella?* As she walked up to the large gate that kept the "haves" protected from the "have nots," she thought of the alarming contrast in the city she had grown to love. Lena had told her that at the most recent count, there were almost seven thousand homeless people in San Francisco. One thousand of those were people under the age of eighteen. As she considered the rain, Amy's heart hurt for those people. The realization in the change of her awareness made her smile. She loved the effect Lena was having on her.

Amy rang the buzzer at the gate, and a very large, very muscular, very angry looking man came to the gate. He was dressed in all black, which Amy felt was a little cliché, but who was she to point that out? He didn't ask for her name, and when he opened the gate, Amy tried to identify herself, but he simply said he knew who she was, and to follow him inside.

The house was incredible, as she expected it would be from the outside. Incredible, except for the fact that it looked like there had been a kegger the night before. Lisa Reynolds was sitting on the couch in a robe. She apparently couldn't be bothered with getting dressed that morning. Her hair looked greasy, and there were still remnants of her makeup clinging to her cheeks and eyelids. Empty bottles lay strewn on the white carpet at her feet. *Rough night.*

"Mrs. Reynolds?" Amy walked over and stood next to her.

Reynolds looked up and gave Amy a convincing and practiced eye roll and look of disdain. "What do you want?" Her voice was cracked, and it sounded like she had either been crying for hours or had just smoked a pack of cigarettes.

For all Amy knew, it could have been both. "I wanted to talk to you about Mr. Reynolds."

She sipped her reddish colored drink. Amy assumed it was tomato juice with an impressive amount of vodka. Amy could smell it from where she was standing.

"What are you here to cover for now?"

"I don't know what you mean." Amy was using a long practiced technique of fishing for information. Peter Reynolds could be up to more than she was aware, and Amy needed to find out everything.

She gave a fake, single syllable laugh. "Did he get caught screwing another tramp?" She looked Amy up and down. "Did he?"

"I wasn't actually aware of any affairs."

"Then you're as blind and as stupid as I was."

Amy felt sorry for her. This woman was clearly in a great deal of pain. But she was here for her client. "I actually came to speak with you about some of the messages you've been posting on Twitter."

"Let me guess. You need me to shut up. Well, it isn't going to happen."

Amy was going to need a different approach. "Can I ask you something?" Amy took her lack of response as a sign to keep speaking. "Are you planning on leaving him?"

"What does it matter to you?" The massive man from the gate brought her another drink, and she took it, barely acknowledging him.

"Well, if you are, you're going about it the wrong way."

Lisa took another sip. "Did you know he's fucking little girls now?"

Amy closed her eyes. She wasn't aware of any evidence that supported her claim. She was sure that if Laura had, in fact, been sleeping with Peter Reynolds, Lena would have a restraining order out on him and he'd be sitting in jail for statutory rape. Still, she felt sick to her stomach. She needed to keep talking. "The Miners made the playoffs. ESPN says they're favored to go all the way to the Super Bowl. That means a very large bonus for their biggest star."

She shook her head vehemently. The anger was so thick Amy could feel it from the couch, three feet away. Lisa's knuckles were turning white from holding the glass so tightly. "If I were you, I would put my best face on—"

Lisa scoffed. "You've got to be kidding me."

Amy held up her hand. "Let me finish. Be the loving and supportive wife you've always been. See this season through, and when it's over, leave him. Take the high road, and you'll get a far better settlement."

She stared at Amy for a long time. "I've been with him since high school, you know."

Amy actually did know. It was her business to know every one of her clients and everyone in their lives. She also knew that because they got married right out of high school, there was no prenuptial agreement. "Lisa, I'm going to be very honest with you. I know you're hurting right now. I know the betrayal has cut you to your absolute core. I also know that the best revenge is success and happiness. So, stay with him and continue the charade you're already living in for another month. Start going to therapy, get your head back on straight, and then leave him and take him to court. Doing anything to jeopardize that now would be foolish. If you do anything he could use against you in court that paints you as anything but a loving and supportive wife, it will only hurt you in the long run."

Lisa Reynolds was quiet for a very long time. She chewed on her nails as she seemed to contemplate the idea. Amy knew that at one time this broken woman sitting in front of her was probably very much in love with the asshole she married. She might still be. It didn't matter though. She felt betrayed, and Peter continued to do things that betrayed that trust and chipped away at his wife's loyalty and belief in him. There was no saving this marriage.

She looked up. "Fine. I'll do it your way."

Amy placed her hand on Lisa's shoulder. "It's what is best for you. Think logically, not emotionally. Think like a survivor, not a victim." Lisa nodded, looking sad and defeated. Amy walked past her bodyguard. "I can show myself out."

Amy walked out of the house and back into the rain. She felt like crying. This was a win. Any other day, this would have been a very good thing. Managing a divorce in the world of public opinion wasn't always easy, but this one would be a piece of cake. She'd just disarmed a ticking bomb, and the partners would be happy. *But that's not all I did.* She'd just convinced a woman who was miserable in her marriage, who was being lied to and betrayed on an almost daily basis, to stay for another month because it's what worked best for her client. Sure, there was truth to the fact that Lisa would be better off legally if she didn't make a scene, and she really would get a better settlement if she handled things quietly, but the reality was she'd done her job. She felt dirty. She turned the ringer on her phone back on and saw a text from Lena. *Good luck with your meeting. I'm sure you'll do great.* She put the phone back into her pocket without answering. Talking to Lena would make her feel worse about herself. *But what if she's the only one who can make me feel better?*

❖

Lena was finishing the books to close out the year. Chloe kept hounding her to get an accountant, and since business was good and only getting better, Lena really needed to consider her suggestion. She needed to start thinking about making more investments for her and Laura's benefit. As if she knew Lena had been thinking about her, Chloe appeared in the doorway of her office.

"Where's Laura?" Lena asked.

"It's nice to see you too. Yes, we had a lovely holiday. No, we didn't really miss you. God, you're so arrogant." Chloe smiled as she walked over to Lena's desk and popped a jellybean in her mouth from the dish that sat on the corner.

"You know, if this lawyer thing doesn't work out for you, you should consider a career in stand-up."

"Ya think?"

"No."

"Ugh! Such a buzzkill. Laura is at my mom's house."

"Really?"

"Yup. She wanted to spend some more time with Ben."

"That's...interesting."

Chloe took a seat in the chair across from Lena's desk and continued to eat jellybeans. "I wouldn't worry about it too much. Ben is pretty harmless."

"I'm not worried. Not really. Okay, maybe a little. But I'm more worried for Ben than I am for Laura."

"They'll be fine. They're with my mom. Now…what happened with you and Amy? Give me all the details."

"When have I ever given you ALL the details?"

"Why do you think I'm ever going to stop asking? Now, let's hear it."

Lena knew she had a goofy smile on her face, but she couldn't help it. She also knew it would have been pointless to try to hide how much she liked Amy from Chloe. "We went up to a place she knows to look at stars."

"Oh man, that's like a roofie for you."

"We didn't have sex, but we did sleep together. It was really sweet and kind of wonderful."

"How is it possible that you're actually seeing someone and getting as much action as me?"

"Why are you such a guy sometimes?"

"What's the issue?"

"There isn't an issue. We just decided to take it slow."

"Huh."

"What does 'huh' mean?"

"Well…you're just doing your normal Lena thing."

"What is my normal Lena thing?"

"Where you say you want to take things slow because you're waiting to find what you consider to be a fatal flaw in someone, so you don't have to get too close. Then you can bail without feeling guilty about it."

"I don't do that."

"Yes…you do." Chloe popped another jellybean in her mouth. "You need to get these away from me."

Lena reached across her desk and pulled the dish away. "There." She said it with more venom then she had meant to, but she was angry and a little hurt.

"I didn't really mean for you to take them away." Lena kept staring at her. "I don't know why you're mad, Lee. I'm your best friend. I'm not here to sugarcoat things for you. I'm here to watch out for you."

Lena's anger vanished. "I don't intentionally push people away."

"I know. But you do. Look, I get it. You've been through a lot, you take on a lot, and you're responsible for a lot. But sometimes it's okay to just let go a little bit. You don't need to keep everything under control. Amy isn't going to be perfect. It's an unrealistic expectation, and you shouldn't just sit back and wait to find the imperfections as a reason to keep yourself closed off. We know she's flawed already. The question is, are you willing to take a chance, already knowing that?"

Lena put her head on her desk. "I'm scared."

"I know, but the things that scare us the most are usually the same things that end up being the best things for us."

Lena still had her head on her desk. "When did you start sounding like a fortune cookie?"

Chloe threw her last jellybean at the top of Lena's head. "Someone has to be the voice of reason when you aren't, and unfortunately, that falls on me for some reason."

Lena lifted her head from the desk. She saw the bracelet around Chloe's wrist and they smiled at each other. "You're my person, you know."

Chloe nodded. "I know. And you're mine. Now tell me about the interview."

❖

"You should invite her." This was the fourth time Sarah had said those exact words. There was no one else Amy wanted to spend New Year's Eve with, and it had been years since she actually wanted to share it with someone. Typically, she would find someone around eleven, spend the obligatory few hours with them, and then go back to their place for a bit of release. Uncomplicated and forgettable. Completely unlike the situation with Lena.

"I'm going to invite her."

"Yeah!" Sarah clapped her hands. "Oh! Ask her in a fun way."

Amy really loved having a friend who cared so much about her happiness and overall well-being. She wanted to reciprocate. "I'll make you a deal. I'll ask Lena to the New Year's cruise if you give Matt your answer, which we both know is yes."

Sarah picked up the stress ball that always sat on Amy's desk. She squeezed it in one hand and then the other. "Okay, deal."

Amy chewed on her pen and smiled at her. "Good."

Sarah stood and grabbed Amy's hand. "Let's go shopping."

Amy stumbled up. "When you say shopping—"

Sarah cut her off as they headed out the door. "I mean in your closet. You have a hundred things I could wear."

"Okay, I just need to make a stop first."

❖

Amy and Sarah left the office and drove to Lands End. Sarah looked over at Amy once she had parked the car. "Did you really just bring me with you to ask Lena out for New Year's?"

Amy shrugged. "Well, I didn't want to do it over text, and you said you'd always wanted to come here."

"Yeah, to eat." She got out of the car and followed Amy to the door. "I've always wanted to come here to *eat*."

Amy pulled the door open. "Okay, then we'll eat."

Sarah huffed. "The waitlist for a reservation at this place is like two months."

Amy gave her a mocking look. "I know the owner," she said with a wink.

The restaurant was incredibly busy. Amy mentally reprimanded herself. She should have known better. It was seven at night at one of the most famed locations in the entire city. Lena was probably really busy. She stood up at the front for several minutes, looking around the restaurant, when the hostess came up and greeted her.

"Ms. Kline?" Amy stared at her. "Ms. Michaels wanted me to bring you back."

Sarah murmured softly. "Fancy."

Amy and Sarah followed the hostess through the dining area to a table Lena and Chloe were sitting at. Lena got out of her chair and hugged Amy. "I saw you up front. What are you doing here?" The question wasn't angry or accusatory. It was said with a bit of excitement. Amy's stomach flipped at the thought that Lena had missed spending time with her too.

"I didn't mean to bother you at work. I just wanted to ask you something in person."

"Oh, it's okay. I'm glad you're here."

Amy motioned to Sarah. "I think you remember Sarah."

Lena nodded. "Glad to see you again, under better circumstances." Lena introduced Sarah and Chloe and motioned to the table. "Please, have a seat."

Lena looked amazing. She was in a pair of slacks that were just tight enough around her thighs and butt. Her button-down, baby blue shirt hugged her breasts, and there was a small gap at the buttons. Amy forced herself not to stare. Lena broke up her internal battle to behave in public.

"Can I get you something to eat?"

Sarah opened the menu. "I can't tell you how long I've been waiting to eat here."

Lena's smile sent a wave of palpitations through Amy's chest.

"Please, order whatever you like, on the house."

Chloe started pointing out a few items on the menu to Sarah. Amy felt Lena's hand on hers. "Is everything okay?"

Amy put her free hand on top of the one holding hers. "Yes, very. I just wanted to invite you to something. Come out with me for New Year's Eve? My firm rents out a yacht. There are fireworks and—"

"Yes."

Lena leaned over and kissed her. It was quick, and for anyone not looking, it would have been missed, but to Amy, it spoke volumes. "Yes?"

Lena nodded her head. The look on her face said she didn't understand why Amy was so surprised. "Yes, I will spend New Year's with you. I just need to make sure Laura is accounted for."

Chloe had obviously been listening. "She'll be at my mom's. She and Ben already made plans."

Lena looked confused. "No one asked me."

Chloe shrugged. "I'm sure she assumed you wouldn't have an issue with her sitting on my mom's couch, watching whatever dorky movie my brother has convinced her will be utterly life changing once she's seen it."

Lena grinned and nodded. "She would have assumed correctly."

Chloe nodded. "Uh-huh."

Amy couldn't contain her excitement. She knew she was wearing a massive cheesy smile, but she didn't care. Then she remembered she had work obligations for the next two nights and wouldn't be able to see Lena. The realization was upsetting, and that fact alone was confusing. "I won't be able to see you until then. Work stuff."

Lena gave her a reassuring smile. "That's okay. I'll still be here." A server walked up and whispered in Lena's ear. She got up from the table. "Seriously, order whatever you want. I have to go take care of a few things, but I'll be back to check on you guys."

Amy watched her as she disappeared toward the kitchen.

Chloe kept reading the menu. Amy found that fact slightly amusing, since she knew there was presumably no one besides the staff that had this menu memorized the way Chloe probably did.

"She likes you." Chloe didn't look up from the menu.

Amy waited for her to continue, waiting for the obligatory "hurt my friend and I will kill you" discussion.

"Lena doesn't fall for people, so please make sure your intentions are what they seem to be. I couldn't bear to watch her have to fix her heart again."

"Her last girlfriend did a number on her?"

Chloe put the menu down. "No, her parents. She was never the same, and not just because they passed. I mean, I don't think anyone is ever the same once they lose their parents. But now, she carries the world on her shoulders. Laura and this restaurant are the most important things to her, but she also uses them as a shield to keep everything else out. Please don't ruin her by taking advantage of the only time she's allowed a chink in that armor."

Sarah listened quietly, then returned to her menu, looking thoughtful. Amy was glad she didn't pipe up with anything to defend her. It wouldn't have felt right, given the honesty of Chloe's statement.

The server came over. Each of them took turns pointing to things on the menu. He also brought a bottle of wine, which he opened and poured into each of their glasses.

Amy thought about Chloe's warning. *Is that what I am? Is that how people see me? As someone who takes advantage of people's weaknesses?* "It's not in my plan to be something or someone she regrets."

"Then we won't have an issue." Chloe raised her glass.

The rest of the conversation continued with ease and amusement. Amy really liked Chloe. She was funny, smart, and her love for Lena was apparent, which made Amy like her even more. She was happy to know Lena had someone in her life that so reverently protected her and cared about her.

They'd just ordered dessert when Chloe stood up and waved across the dining area. "Oh good, she made it."

Amy looked across the room to see who she was waving at. *Evelyn.* Amy felt a lump swell in the back of her throat. Her hands tingled, and she had a sudden urge to flee. The room tilted and spun.

Sarah grabbed her arm. "What's wrong? You look like you're going to be sick."

Amy didn't get a chance to respond before Evelyn was standing next to her. Chloe interrupted her panic attack.

"Evelyn is a new hire with my firm. So she's new to the area, and I texted her to see if she wanted to join us. Evelyn, this is Sarah and Amy."

Amy stared at Evelyn, unable to speak past the bile in the back of her throat. She wanted to shake her hand, she wanted to play along, she wanted to be able to show just how far she had come from their time together, but she didn't. She couldn't move.

Evelyn shook Sarah's hand and sat down. "Amy and I actually already know each other."

Chloe looked genuinely surprised. "From where?"

Evelyn looked over at Amy. Amy remembered that look well. She was trying to decide how much to reveal. "We dated in college."

Now it was Chloe's turn to look pale. "Seriously?"

Amy was having trouble breathing. It felt like there was a sumo wrestler slowly sitting on her chest. She didn't know if she was actually sweating or if she just thought she was. Her body was betraying her mind. She felt cold and sweaty, all at once. She needed to get a handle on this situation. *Control it. Fix it. I do this for other people. I can do it for myself.* "We dated for three years and lived together for one."

Evelyn moved her hair out of her eyes. At least being in this situation was making her nervous as well, and Amy wasn't the only one suffering.

Evelyn finally said, "I should go. I didn't want to make this awkward for anyone, and I'm afraid that's what I've done."

Amy saw Lena walking over out of the corner of her eye. The last thing she wanted was for Lena to see her like this. She stood up. "No, you stay. You two work together and probably have a lot to talk about. I needed to head home anyway. I have a lot of work the next few days. I need to get a head start." She was grateful that her professional skills had taken over, allowing her voice to stay smooth and calm, an absolute contrast to what was going on inside of her. For good measure she added, "The food here is excellent. You two enjoy."

Amy managed to make it out of the restaurant, with Sarah following closely behind, before Lena had made it to the table. She didn't say good-bye, but she'd explain later, when she didn't feel like she was about to burst into pieces. It wasn't a conversation she wanted to have in front of anyone, least of all, Evelyn.

The cold air hugged her as soon as the door opened. It was a welcome relief from the suffocation of being in an enclosed space with her ex. The sound of her heart pounding in her head was making her slightly dizzy. She felt a hand on her shoulder and glanced at it, expecting it to be Sarah's. *Nail polish.* She turned around and once again looked into the eyes of the only person that had ever completely annihilated her.

"Amy, I'm sorry." Evelyn had her arms wrapped around herself. She had apparently taken off after her without her jacket.

Amy didn't respond until Sarah had gotten into the car and shut the door. "I don't want to do this with you, Evelyn."

"I know you don't want to do this, but we need to."

"No. We don't."

"Damn it, Amy. You never wanted to talk about anything. You always just thought it would go away on its own."

"That's not true." Amy couldn't believe she was going to accuse her of anything, not after what she'd done.

"Don't you think I wanted to talk to you before I left? That I wanted to explain things?"

Amy gave a mocking laugh. "Don't do that. Don't try to put that on me. You didn't tell me because that was easier for you. You only do what is easiest for you."

"That's not true. I didn't tell you because I knew you would be hurt, angry, and you wouldn't have listened."

"Jesus, Evelyn! I was entitled to be all those things. You were leaving me without any warning. We made plans. We had a future. We had even named our children, for Christ's sake. Then I come home to find you with some bullshit note in your hand. You decided to blow the whole thing up, without any warning, without giving us a chance to work out whatever issues you had decided made us unfixable. And some of the things you said before you left…"

"I was young and selfish. I thought it would be easier on everyone in the long run."

"Easier? Do you have any idea what I've become because of that day?"

Evelyn didn't say anything. She stared at Amy, and for the first time, Amy saw something she had missed the last time she saw her. There was hurt, sadness, and fear in her expression. She hated to acknowledge that Evelyn could have some basis for what she'd said. "You broke my heart."

"I know."

"You broke it and never looked back. You changed your phone number. I couldn't talk to you. I couldn't tell you what you had done to me. You just took off and left me to pick up the pieces. I had to wake up every day in that crappy apartment we had picked out together. I had to watch television on that ugly couch you picked out. I had to take down all our pictures. I had to do all of that, and you just started over without giving me a second thought."

"I thought about you every day."

"If that's true, why didn't you call me?"

"Because I didn't think you would ever want to hear from me again."

"That may be the only thing you ever got right about me."

"Don't do that, Amy. Don't minimize our entire relationship to one action, one day, one decision."

"One decision? That one decision ended our entire relationship!"

Evelyn was starting to get frustrated now. Her hands came down by her sides, her anger apparently fighting off the cold. "Okay, Amy, yes, I hurt you. Yes, I left you. No, I didn't give you a choice in it. I made the decision for both of us. But can you honestly tell me that you would still want to be with me? That you would have taken the job you did if it wasn't for us breaking up? Would you still be here if it wasn't for that hard decision I made? No. You wouldn't have. You would've followed me to law school and you would've worked somewhere you hated. You would have settled to keep me happy. I wasn't going to let you do that, so I made the decision. I'm sorry I hurt you. I'm sorrier than I can ever explain, but we both know I did the right thing."

Amy was in shock. She had never considered things from that point of view. Evelyn leaving had made it possible for her to be here, in the city she loved, and the job she'd worked her ass off at. She had spent so much time blaming her, she'd never considered all the good that came from it. "You're right."

Evelyn was getting ready to argue again, but Amy's response stopped her. "What?"

"You're right. I would have followed you anywhere. And I wouldn't have been happy."

Evelyn took Amy's hands. They were ice cold, but she still wasn't shivering. "I am sorry I hurt you. And if it makes a difference, it was because I loved you."

"You weren't in love with me anymore, though, were you?" Amy asked the question, even though she knew the answer. She needed to hear it out loud.

Evelyn looked like she was going to cry. "No, I wasn't. I wanted to be, but I wasn't. I did love you though, and I will always love you."

She hugged Amy. The immediate and unexpected contact caught her off guard, and she wasn't sure how to feel about it. But in that instant, she also felt a weight she'd been carrying for far too long fall from her shoulders. "I forgive you." She meant it. Something she never thought would be possible, and yet, it was true.

Evelyn continued to hug her. "Thank you."

"You're welcome. And I'm sorry too."

Evelyn took a step back. "Do you think we could get coffee sometime?"

Amy nodded. "I'd like that." She handed her a business card from the purse she had finally stopped clutching like a life preserver.

Evelyn walked back into the warm reprieve of Lands End, and Amy turned to the car. Life had changed, rapidly, and she needed some time to process. Her phone rang and she sighed. *No rest for the wicked. After work, anyway.*

Lena stood in front of Chloe, holding on to the chair next to her. Chloe explained that Amy, Sarah, and Evelyn had disappeared out the front door after it was revealed that Evelyn and Amy had dated in college. Lena wanted to go after Amy, but was also a little worried about what she would find. It wasn't difficult to put the pieces together. Evelyn was Evie. Evie, the woman who had forged Amy's heart into what it was today. Was this the love of Amy's life that had just walked back into her orbit by the means of the front doors to Lands End?

"She didn't say anything else?"

Chloe sipped her wine. "I'm only going to tell you one more time, and then you're either going to go find out for yourself, or go supervise something in the kitchen. They said they dated in college and Amy said she had to go because of work."

"And she looked upset?"

"She looked upset, but she didn't sound upset." Chloe put her wine glass down. "I like Amy, well, from what I know of her, that is. But she seems to have a lot of baggage."

"I don't think an ex-girlfriend counts as baggage. We all have exes."

"Then why are you so worried?"

"That's the woman that sent Amy off the deep end."

"What does that mean?"

"Amy has been with a lot of women, all because of a broken heart. Evelyn is patient zero, so to speak."

"Fabulous."

Lena watched as Evelyn came gliding across the dining area. She was stunning. Her dark, perfect skin tone matched her copper eyes. She was tall, almost Lena's height, and carried herself as if she had a few inches on top of that. Her high heels matched her purse, which matched her watch. Lena wanted to straighten out her own shirt but didn't want to seem intimidated. Not to mention, she didn't want to draw attention to the few food stains on it. So instead, she stood still, statue-like.

Evelyn took her seat. "I'm so sorry about that. We needed to have a talk, one we should have had years ago." She looked up at Lena and put out her hand. "Hi. I'm Evelyn. I'm sure Chloe has probably caught you up by now." She added a smile at the end.

Damn it. Perfect teeth, too. Lena wanted to wipe her hand on her pants before shaking her hand, but didn't want to seem so uncouth. "Lena."

Evelyn smiled. "Yes, I know who you are. Chloe speaks about you often."

Lena glanced over at Chloe, who managed a shy shrug. "So what happened?"

Leave it to Chloe to get straight to the point. *I love you, Chloe.* Lena tried to look politely interested, rather than desperate.

Evelyn picked up her glass of untouched wine. Even her fingers were perfect. They were long and elegant, with a single golden ring on her middle finger. Lena had never even paid attention to fingers before, but she was transfixed.

"I had never given Amy the chance to say how I had affected her. We finally cleared the air. It's good though. We're going to have coffee in the near future."

Perfect.

Chloe leaned forward on the table. She raised her eyebrows. "Oh? Do you think there's a chance you two will get back together?"

Evelyn sipped her wine as she looked between Lena and Chloe. "I hadn't thought about it. I doubt it, though. There are some hurts that you do to people that can never be undone. She says she forgives me, but I don't think she would ever be able to move past it."

"Do you want to?" The words jumped out of Lena's mouth when she had intended for them to stay inside her head, along with all of the other thoughts that were hopping around up there. Like: How is it possible to sustain that level of flawless hair on a daily basis, and is that lip gloss or are your lips really that perfect?

Evelyn shook her head as if she was trying to dislodge an abrupt thought. "I don't even know if she's single. We didn't have a chance to talk about it."

"She's dating Lena." Chloe could always be counted on for subtlety and a practical approach for disseminating information.

Lena felt totally exposed. She didn't actually know if they were dating. They had been on a date, to be exact. The other times they'd spent together…well, she didn't know how to classify them. Did that mean they were dating? "We've been out once."

Chloe interrupted again. "And you're going out on New Year's."

"Yes. And we're going out on New Year's." She had said it much quieter than she had intended. Evelyn made her incredibly uneasy.

Evelyn took another sip of her wine. Lena knew by the way she was looking at her, she was doing mental calculations, and Lena was being studied. She hated it. Luckily, one of the staff was trying to get her attention from right outside the kitchen. "Excuse me." She quickly walked across the dining area to the safety of the stainless steel doors.

Chapter Fourteen

Amy stared out the expansive window of her office. She had her telephone earpiece in, the one she'd always sworn she would never wear, because it reminded her of douchey Wall Street brokers. Yet, here she was. Earpiece in, listening to an irate man searching for every derogatory adjective he could think of to describe his business competition.

While he was ranting, she pushed the button on her phone to look for a text notification. There wasn't one. There hadn't been one all day, in fact. Well, that wasn't entirely true; there just hadn't been one from Lena. "Yes, Mr. Manning. I understand what you're saying, but I can't just run ads saying he's a liar." She continued her intensive examination of the pants she was wearing, picking pieces of lint off them. It was safe to say she had been almost as effective as a lint roller. "If you have actual proof that he stole your idea, we can move forward."

Sarah walked in and dumped more files on her desk. Amy held up her hand and made the motion of a mouth talking with her hand. "Yes, Mr. Manning, I look forward to hearing back from you then." She pulled the piece out of her ear and tossed it on her desk.

"Manning accusing Williams of stealing his furniture designs again?"

Amy opened the files that Sarah had dropped on her desk. "Yes. I still don't understand why he thinks he has the market cornered on chairs." She pointed to a line in the file. "Are these today's tweets?"

Sarah looked over her shoulder. "Yes. Lisa Reynolds seems to be following your advice."

"Good."

"You know, you could always create a Twitter account and check these yourself."

Amy shook her head. "Then what would you do with all that free time?"

Sarah picked the file up. "I can't even imagine."

Amy's phone pinged and she picked it up quickly, hoping it was from Lena. "Evelyn again."

"What does it say?"

"She wants to meet for coffee after work. Do people have coffee after work? I thought it was usually drinks."

Sarah crossed her arms. "Do you want it to be drinks?"

Amy ignored the question. "I can't anyway. I have a dinner thing with the partners."

"You deflected that answer with no problem."

"Have you told Matt your answer yet?"

Sarah got up to walk out of the room. "Nicely done, again."

The truth was, Amy didn't want to spend time with anyone but Lena. Having drinks, or coffee, with Evelyn wasn't something she wanted to do, even if they'd decided on a truce of sorts. She hadn't heard from Lena today, and the vague sense of insecurity it caused made her feel even more uneasy. She'd never cared if a woman called again, and the fact that she cared now was more than a little unnerving.

Sarah beeped in on the speakerphone. "You could always call her."

Amy pushed the button. "Thanks, Dr. Phil. Stay out of my head."

Amy couldn't see Sarah's face from where she sat, but she knew her well enough to know she'd rolled her eyes.

❖

Lena sat with Laura at an empty table. Laura was dressed in her hostess uniform. Black slacks, a button-down white shirt, with her hair pulled back. She picked up her phone and smiled as her fingers tapped furiously on the keyboard. "Are you talking to Ben?"

Laura took a deep breath and then put her phone down. "Yes."

Getting information out of Laura was probably as frustrating as interrogating a prisoner. "Are you spending the New Year with him?"

"Yes." Laura crossed her arms.

"You guys are staying at Tina's though, right?" Lena tried to keep her voice level and calm, in an attempt to not incite the crazy teenage beast that was dormant for the time being.

"Yes."

"Do you know any other words?"

"I'm answering your questions. If you want more information, ask something that requires more than a one syllable response."

There it is. She sighed inwardly. "Okay. What will you two be doing?"

"We're going to get drunk and have sex."

"Laura!"

"What? You ask ridiculous questions. Tina and David will be there. We're eating dinner and watching movies."

"Why can't you just say that?"

"And pass up the opportunity to get you all pissy? Not gonna happen. What are you doing, anyway?"

Lena sat back in her chair and stared at her. This was one of the rare opportunities she had to actually have a sisterly conversation with her and not act like her mom. She should take advantage. "I'm going out with Amy."

Laura smiled. "You going to get drunk and have sex?"

"Knock it off."

Laura was laughing. "You need to loosen up. Maybe that's exactly what you should do."

Lena was going to answer, but she saw Brittany at the front door. She leaned across the table. "Are you sure you're okay with this?"

Laura also looked at the front door, where Brittany was standing. "Yeah, I'll be fine. Maybe it will help."

"Okay, but if there's anything you don't want to answer, you don't have to. Are you sure you don't want me in there with you?"

Laura stared at her with a look that implied she should know the answer. "Yes. I'm very sure." At Lena's skeptical look, she said, "I promise, I'll be fine."

Lena had to take her word for it. "Okay. You can stop the interview at any time, though. It ends if you get uncomfortable. Got it?" She waited for Laura to nod, and noticed the way she was pushing at her cuticles. She was nervous, no matter how cool she was trying to play it.

Brittany was in black leather. Again. Lena forced herself not to ask if she owned anything else. Instead, she got up and shook her hand and then introduced her to Laura. "You two can use my office." They walked toward the back, and Lena fought every urge to follow them with a glass to put up to the door.

Instead of channeling her inner NSA agent, she pulled out her phone and looked at it again. Amy had texted her that morning, and she hadn't responded yet. It was childish, but she was jealous of the woman from the other night, and she didn't even know if there was reason to be. The grownup thing to do would be to ask what the situation with Evelyn was. But then, that could come off as clingy and neurotic. *Better not to say anything. Just see what happens.* Lena justified her actions by reminding herself that she didn't really know Amy. They'd only known each other for a few weeks. She didn't *need* to text her back. If she had some unfinished business with an ex, then who was she to stand in the way of it? She thought back to Chloe's assertion that she pushed people away, and intentionally ignored it.

Over an hour later, Lena was busy doing a midweek inventory in the back stockroom when Laura walked in and touched her arm. Lena pulled out her headphones. "What's up?"

Laura looked emotionally drained, and Lena forced herself not to hug her, unsure if it was something Laura wanted. *When did I start worrying about whether or not I could hug my own sister?* The thought made her incredibly sad.

"Brittany is waiting in the dining room." Laura managed a half smile and squeezed Lena's shoulder as she walked past.

Brittany stood with her hands in her pockets, surrounded by an aura of coolness that seemed to follow her every movement. "Thanks again, Lena. I really appreciate it."

"I hope it helps. It would be great to put this behind us, once and for all."

Brittany nodded. "I hope so, too. The story should run on the first of January. I'm going to do a few more interviews today and tomorrow. I have appointments lined up with the officers that were first on the scene and the investigating detectives. They were actually pretty eager to help."

Lena hadn't expected for it to be that fast. She also wasn't sure if Brittany would be able to do her parents justice with that brief timeline. Brittany seemed to sense her apprehension.

"I plan to keep following up on this story, until we're able to get to the bottom of it."

"Even if the first article doesn't turn up any other information?"

Brittany smiled. "Even then. It bothers me that this guy has been out there for so long. Doesn't seem right. "

"Thank you, Brittany."

"Do you want me to send it to you before it's printed?"

Lena thought about it for a minute. In truth, part of her wanted it all to stay in the shadows, so she wouldn't have to deal with it. But maybe it was time to let go and see what would happen. "No, I trust you. I don't think you'd write anything unprofessional."

"Glad to hear it. Okay, I'll be in touch." She walked out the front door.

Lena wondered, for what must have been the millionth time, if she had made the right decision. This story was going to thrust her and her sister back into the spotlight, and the world was a very different place now. Bloggers and social media seemed to dictate the news cycle. People gave instant feedback on every situation from the safety of their anonymous keyboards. She briefly considered calling Brittany and asking her not to print the story, but stopped herself. Laura wasn't a little girl anymore, and this was something that hung over both their heads, even if they went weeks or months without mentioning it. If there was a chance that any type of closure could occur, it was worth a shot.

Chapter Fifteen

On New Year's Eve, Lena stood in front of the mirror, second-guessing everything. She'd eventually texted Amy back, after thinking about how suddenly life could change, and although their texts had been a little cooler, they'd still agreed to go out tonight, and she was glad. She'd wanted to slow things down, and the weird meeting with Amy's ex had helped on that front. It was, maybe, a little disappointing, but she knew it was right. She'd tried to ignore the slightly hurt tone in Amy's texts, figuring it would all be okay again once they spent more time together in person. Chloe sat on Lena's bed and flipped through the music channels on the television while Lena fixed the sleeves on her jacket. It was the nicest outfit she owned. She'd had it tailored to fit her perfectly about a year prior, for an awards banquet she had attended for Chloe. The black Hugo Boss suit had cost her more than she had ever spent on any piece of clothing, but it was worth every penny. It fit perfectly across her shoulders and waist, and the black shirt she wore under was snug, leaving no bulges under the jacket. The bright white tie was a great contrast.

"Hopefully, you don't spill anything on the tie this time." Chloe was leaning back in the bed, watching her get dressed.

"As I remember, you spilled on me." Lena continued to look in the mirror, now second-guessing the white. "Should I wear something else?"

"Nope. The white works perfectly with that suit. You look stunning."

"You think?"

"I do. She won't be able to keep her hands off you."

"What are you doing tonight?"

"I'm not doing anything. Don't change the subject. That's what you want, right? To be irresistible?"

"I told you, we're taking things slow."

"And I told you that's a cop-out. What's going on with you?"

Lena adjusted her tie again in the mirror. "You've seen the women she's been with."

Chloe walked over and stood next to Lena in the mirror. "Have you seen you?"

Lena leaned on the counter, staring at herself in the mirror. "Brittany is ridiculously cool. She exudes 'badass.' Evelyn is quite possibly one of the most gorgeous women I've ever seen, and those are just the two I've met."

"Is that why you've been so weird about this?"

"I don't know."

"If you honestly think you aren't in the same league as those women, you're high."

Lena gave her a sideways look. "I hate that saying."

Chloe ignored her comment and continued. "Amy clearly has a thing for gorgeous women, and you fit right in. The difference is, you're attractive without even trying."

"You have to say that; you're my best friend."

"That may be true, but what I'm saying also happens to be completely factual."

"What if there's still something between her and Evelyn?"

Chloe turned Lena to look at her and put her hands on her face. "That's for Amy to decide. Not for you to make up weird scenarios in your head and then push her away because you've convinced yourself she's a villain of some kind."

"We have only known each other for like, three weeks. It's too soon."

Chloe kissed her forehead. "She came and helped at Lands End, you went over and had dinner with her on Christmas, you went out on a date, and she came in person to ask you out for New Year's. In the lesbian world, doesn't that mean you're practically engaged?" She playfully smacked Lena's cheek.

"That's a terrible stereotype."

Chloe laughed. "Seriously, there's no appropriate time frame. Stop trying to shove everything into an organized box and just let it happen. If it's right, it's right. And if it's wrong, then it will suck and we'll get over it together with wine and ice cream."

"So, there's no plan."

"That's the plan."

"You're really annoying sometimes. I love you."

Amy stared in the mirror. This was the fourth dress she had put on. Technically, it was the first she'd tried on, and she'd finally circled back to it. Simple, black, elegant. She looked at herself from a side angle for what seemed like the hundredth time. She was looking in the mirror, but her mind was elsewhere. She had only had the chance to speak with Lena off and on the last few days over text, and those texts had felt decidedly different. Work had been crazy, as she'd prepped for the Uber Technologies meeting and dealt with a thousand other issues that came up. She'd had drinks or dinner with the partners and clients the last few nights, and then fallen asleep the moment her head had hit the pillow. Normally, she thrived in this type of work environment. She loved the fast-paced world her job offered, but it wasn't the same these last few days. She looked at her clients in a slightly different light. While she had been out for drinks, a client had leaned over and showed her a picture of himself with a woman that wasn't his wife, in a compromising position, that had been texted to him earlier that day. This was an easy fix, and cheating, unfortunately, wasn't a novelty, nor did he seem in any way ashamed of it.

She was able to make the photo go away between sips of her drink with just a few text messages and a rather small deposit into a PayPal account. She had reached a level of proficiency she had always hoped to achieve. But instead of feeling accomplished, she was a bit ashamed. Staring at herself in the mirror wasn't helping to diminish those feelings.

The other part of it was because Lena had been a bit standoffish; they seemed to go from fiery hot to lukewarm. Well, Lena had become lukewarm. Amy still wanted her, thought about her no matter what she was doing, burned for her. For the life of her, she couldn't figure out what she had done wrong, but she intended to correct it tonight.

The firm Amy worked at, Morgan & Morgan, sent a car for every person who attended their New Year's party. It was their generous way of avoiding any type of drinking and driving incidents, and thereby isolating any potential media risks. She asked the driver to take her to Lena's, and in a few short minutes, the car sat in front of her house. Amy looked down at the book she had purchased, unsure whether or not to bring it up to the door, or give it to her in the car. Amy wasn't used to doing things like this, bringing gifts on dates. She didn't date, and the more time she spent getting to know Lena, the more she realized how out of practice she was. *Oh God. Do people give books as gifts? Should I have brought wine instead? Donuts? Diamonds?* She shook her head and took a deep breath. *Calm down. It's a frigging book.*

She decided to take it to the door so Lena could leave it inside. She walked up the path to the doorway, noticing the heaviness of the air. The rain was holding off for now, but it would be coming down later. Hopefully, she'd either still be enjoying the party, or enjoying the sound of it from beneath the covers. *And not alone.* The door opened before she had a chance to knock. "Hi, Chloe."

Chloe looked her up and down. Thankfully, it was a look of appreciation and not revulsion. Amy wasn't sure what reception she'd get after the way she'd left the restaurant. And if Evelyn and Chloe were friends, she had no idea what Evelyn might have said about her.

"You look beautiful, Amy."

Amy walked inside. "Thank you. I'm sorry about the other night—"

Chloe held up her hand. "I'm sorry. I honestly had no idea."

"There was no way you could have."

Lena came down the stairs but stopped when she saw Amy. Lena's cheeks turned a little flushed as she blatantly looked her over, and Amy felt relieved. The heat was still there. Lena looked phenomenal. Her suit was exquisite, making Amy want to remove it from her. "You look amazing." Lena finally made it over to her and Amy kissed her cheek, taking a second to breathe in the lovely scent she'd come to associate with Lena. She ran her hand over Amy's bare back, sending chills through every part of her.

"You look beautiful."

"Thank you. I umm…I got you something." Amy held out the book a little awkwardly. Lena took it and flipped it over to inspect the cover.

"*The Complete Guide to the Constellations.* Thank you. That's incredibly thoughtful."

"Well, you two are adorable, but I need to go to my mom's to eat my body weight in pizza, just to ensure I stay single forever and never have to live through something so perfect myself." Chloe grabbed her jacket off the chair and left after giving Lena a quick kiss on the cheek.

Amy laughed as Chloe left. "She's funny."

"Yes, but don't tell her. It goes to her head."

"I'll remember that."

If it were up to Amy, they wouldn't go anywhere tonight. They would stay right here and she would slowly and carefully remove the dapper suit Lena was wearing, piece by piece. She looked up into those blue eyes, contemplating posing that very question, when Lena took her hand.

"You ready to go?"

"Yes, let's." That wasn't true, but anywhere with Lena was better than doing anything with anyone else.

Lena felt like she had been dropped straight into a romantic movie. Amy was breathtaking, and the thoughtfulness of the gift had taken her a bit by surprise. Now they sat in a sleek black car, on the way to a yacht for a New Year's Eve celebration. The San Francisco weather played its part, with the rainy mist and cold weather. She couldn't remember the last time her chest had burned with excitement and happiness the way it was in this moment.

"So, this is a work party, but there are clients and contractors there too. The food is normally incredible, and it's open bar, which is always a plus."

Lena took Amy's hand. She could barely make out her face in the dark, but the city lights flashing by were enough to accentuate her beautiful features. "I'm looking forward to it."

Amy smiled, and Lena's chest burned hotter. They had barely been together for a few minutes, but Lena knew if she continued to feel like she did right now, it was going to be one of the best nights of her life. She was going to take Chloe's advice and enjoy it, instead of thinking fifteen steps ahead.

The car slowed a few minutes later as a string of vehicles stopped to let out the occupants. People were boarding a massive yacht, with about four levels. Lena muttered softly, "Wow," as she exited the car and pulled on her jacket.

"One more thing. I've never taken anyone to an event, so you may get a few strange looks. I assure you, it's not because of you, and has everything to do with me."

"Haven't you worked there for a long time?" Lena was surprised Amy wouldn't have brought any number of women as a date.

"I tend to keep my personal life and my professional life separate. And when you bring someone to something like this, there's a kind of...expectation, I guess, that something more is possible." She shrugged slightly, a slight grin suggesting tonight meant just that.

Lena's heart fluttered as Amy took her hand and they headed up the large metal walkway that ended on the enormous, fantastic boat.

There was a sign as they entered, explaining what each level was for: gallery, dining, dancing, and the viewing deck. A young man in a tuxedo took their coats as they walked up, in exchange for a small ticket with a number. Amy stuck both in her purse. They hadn't taken another five steps before they were greeted by two men who appeared to be in their late sixties. Amy introduced Lena without ever letting go of her hand, an observation she savored. The two men were the grandsons of the original Morgan & Morgan, and looked like the type who came from money. They wore their suits like they had been born in them. They exuded class and a level of comfort that was distinguishable even from the other people around them. Amy had the same type of subtle sophistication to her. It could come across as arrogance, but with Amy, it was sensual. Lena thought her confidence was sexy, and even in this sea of tailored suits and fake smiles, genuine.

As Amy and Lena walked through the gallery, numerous people held up their glasses in an acknowledgment to Amy. She seemed almost embarrassed by the attention, and she never let go of Lena's hand. They reached a tall cocktail table where Sarah and a very good-looking man were standing.

"Lena, you already know Sarah, but this is her—"

"Matt is my fiancé." Sarah beamed as Matt put his arm around her.

"Well, it's about time," Amy said as she hugged them both.

"Matt is a detective." Sarah's pride in him was obvious.

Lena put her hand out and took Matt's. "It is very nice to meet you, Matt."

Matt's smile was welcoming, genuine, and charming. "It's very nice to meet you, Lena."

"Apparently, congratulations are in order?"

Matt smiled again and even managed to turn a little red, and Lena instantly liked him.

"She finally said yes. I couldn't be happier." He smiled down at Sarah before he continued. "And may I add that you all look phenomenal tonight. I am by far the luckiest guy in the room, to be sitting with you three tonight." Sarah kissed his cheek and he pulled her closer.

Some less romantic people would have found their behavior nauseating. Lena, however, wasn't one of those people. Matt and Sarah were clearly a part of an elite club, a club that her father had referred to as the "lucky ones." They weren't just in love; it was clear they were partners, best friends, teammates. Lena found it reassuring and refreshing when she encountered couples like this. It meant true love did exist, and it was obtainable. She didn't know them, but she was truly happy for them.

Sarah asked, "What would you like to drink, Lena? Amy and I will go grab this round. The servers always dote on the clients at these events, so we could wait hours for one to come by for us."

Matt stood up a little straighter. "Are you sure you don't want me to go?"

"Yes. We need to talk about you two." She kissed him again on the cheek. "That's always more fun when you're not there."

"I like red wine, thank you."

Amy squeezed Lena's hand and then disappeared into the crowd of waiting, thirsty partygoers. Lena knew she was smiling as Amy walked away, but she didn't care.

Matt broke the silence. "This is my third one of these, and I don't think I'll ever get comfortable at them."

Lena looked around. "It is really impressive. You mean the police department doesn't spring for these types of events?"

"Ha! They don't even pay for our lunches when we have staff meetings."

Lena laughed and tried to focus on him, rather than staring at the crowd waiting for Amy to come back. "So you're a detective, huh? That must be fascinating."

"It's actually a lot more paperwork than I ever imagined." He chuckled. "But I do enjoy it. I'm new on the job so I do a lot of shadowing right now. Shadowing and cold cases."

Lena wasn't sure if she should ask, but she wanted to know the answer, and her instincts told her there weren't a lot of coincidences in her world right now. "Cold cases? Any chance you're assigned to the task of looking into my parents' case?"

Matt nodded. "Kind of. Brittany contacted me. I met her around this time last year, through Sarah and Amy, on another case they were caught up in with some celebrity. I told her I can't officially reopen anything until my captain tells me to, but I assume with the story coming out, it won't be long now."

Lena didn't know if the idea made her happy, nervous, or concerned. She wanted closure. She and Laura both needed it. But she was also concerned about the possible fallout. She wasn't sure if the unknown was better than the truth, but that didn't make much sense.

"I promise you, Lena, I'm not in it for any type of publicity. I genuinely want to help figure out what happened. I've read a lot about that night. I'd like to be involved, if I can."

Surprisingly, Lena was grateful that Matt would be the one working on it. She didn't know him at all, but there was something about him that made her feel comfortable. "Thank you."

A few more minutes passed, and Sarah and Amy came back to the table, drinks in hand. "Whatever he told you about me is completely untrue." Amy smiled at Matt.

"That's too bad, since he just told me you're the kindest, smartest, most wonderful woman he knows, next to Sarah."

"Now I know you're a liar. Matt wouldn't say that."

Lena wrapped her arm around Amy. "No. But if he had, you would have felt really silly right now."

A few minutes later, it was announced that dinner would be served on the second floor and for everyone to please go up and find their seats. Amy took Lena's hand, and they followed the droves of people up an incredible set of spiral stairs. Lena enjoyed watching Amy move, and it wasn't just because of the dress, although that was a definite plus. She was graceful, confident, and beautiful. She smiled and waved at numerous people, making eye contact long enough with each person to ensure they felt seen. It was a quality her father had perfected as well, and Lena enjoyed seeing it in someone else. Lena hadn't known what to expect when she had agreed to come to Amy's work party. A part of her was scared she would be a completely different person, soulless, apathetic. Fake, perhaps. But Amy wasn't any of those things. Sure, she seemed focused and attentive to who was around, but she was still Amy. The Amy, she realized, she had fallen for.

Matt and Sarah were funny, animated, and a pleasure to be around. Their easy conversation made Lena feel welcome and like they had been friends for years. She was also acutely aware of Amy's hand on her leg, rubbing small circles and inching upward. Lena was starting to struggle to pay attention to the conversation. Her leg was tingling in the spot where Amy's hand teased her. The tingling spread throughout her whole body. It was intoxicating and invigorating all at the same time. It had been a long time since a simple and intimate touch had affected her so thoroughly.

Lena watched carefully as Amy laughed. Her eyes glowed when she was amused. Her whole being radiated with joy. It was incredible; Amy was incredible. She leaned over, to insinuate that she needed to whisper something. Amy leaned over, and Lena put her mouth up to her ear. "I don't think I've ever seen anything more beautiful than you." Amy pressed her cheek to Lena's and let it linger there for a moment, their skin touching. Amy was warm, and the faint hint of her perfume from behind her ear urged Lena to kiss her. Lena forgot she was in a room, surrounded by hundreds of strangers, and for a moment, there was nothing but Amy. Until there wasn't.

"Amy, hi."

She recognized the voice, the one that sounded like it had been woven out of pure silk. The woman was flawless, and tonight was no exception. Lena hated how self-conscious she suddenly felt.

"Hello, Evelyn." Amy's tone was even, her smile polite.

Lena saw Sarah dig her hand into Matt's arm. Matt looked around, clearly trying to figure out what was going on. Evelyn stood in front of the table, one hand on her hip, the other loosely holding an expensive looking clutch. Her sheer blue gown looked like it probably cost more than Lena spent on clothes in an entire year. Her dark, bronzed skin showed no sign of age or imperfections. She had apparently been born into some type of bubble she was allowed to live in her whole life, just being perfect and flawless.

"What are you doing here?" Amy's voice was kind, but there was an edge to it.

"I'm here with Greg." She waved over to another table to prove she wasn't some stowaway. "Plans with his girlfriend fell through, he had an extra ticket, and I happened to be free."

Luckily, there was a straight woman at the table, immune to Evelyn's polarizing looks. "How do you know Greg Sampson?" Sarah's tone was a little harsh and a tad accusatory.

Lena really liked Sarah. She assumed the person in question had some kind of celebrity status, since he didn't look like the type to work in an office.

"My firm represents him. I'm assigned to his account." She smiled at Sarah.

"Lovely." Sarah let go of Matt and crossed her arms.

"You look beautiful tonight, Amy." Evelyn's tone was sincere, which was irritating, and the fact that it was irritating, made it even more irritating. She did her best not to roll her eyes at her own reflections.

"Thank you." Amy's light grasp on Lena's leg intensified. The problem was, Lena didn't know if she wanted to be closer, or if she needed to be grounded in Evelyn's presence. *At least she didn't return the compliment. That's something, right?*

Evelyn nodded toward the table with her date. "Amy, would you mind coming over and saying hello to Greg? He actually asked me to come over and grab you."

Amy turned and looked at Lena. There was an apology in her eyes "Greg is one of our biggest clients. I have to go over there, I'm sorry."

Lena removed her hand from Amy's. "Of course. You should go." That's not what Lena was thinking and it definitely wasn't what she was feeling, but it came out of her mouth all the same.

❖

Amy walked over to the table where Greg sat, a fake smile plastered to her face. It was irritating that Evelyn was here in general, and now she was pulling her away, intentionally, from her date with Lena. Talking to clients was part of her job, but talking to them with her ex-girlfriend wasn't something she'd anticipated.

She glanced back over at her table. Sarah, Matt, and Lena were leaning toward one another, probably talking about the scene that just unfolded. She needed to get this over with quickly.

"Greg, hi!" Amy kissed his cheek as he stood to greet her.

"Amy, it's nice to see you. I'm sorry I pulled you away from your evening. I just wanted to catch you." They both sat down.

"I have a situation I'm going to need you to handle." He went on to explain in far greater detail than she needed to hear about a sexual situation he'd gotten himself into. Amy watched his lips move and listened to the ridiculousness that came out of his mouth. *Men in power. It's like they've got carte blanche to do whatever they want.* The funny thing was, they did, because there were people like Amy to smooth out their egregious behavior. It made her feel…dirty.

It took about fifteen minutes to hear the entire situation, one he obviously wasn't as embarrassed about as he should be, since he made no effort to keep his voice down. Amy assured him she'd take care of it and not to worry. She wanted this conversation to be over. It was getting close to midnight, and she wanted to be with Lena. She said her good-byes and made a move to get up from the table. Evelyn put her hand on top of hers. "Can we talk?"

Amy looked back over at her table and Lena was gone. Obviously, she couldn't have gone far, since they were floating about a half a mile from the shore. But her absence worried her. "About what, Evelyn?"

"We haven't gotten together for that coffee."

Amy knew the look Evelyn was giving her. She'd seen it a hundred times before. The only difference was that this time, she felt nothing.

"Evelyn, I agreed to have coffee because we're clearly going to continue to run into each other." She lowered her voice to make sure no one else could hear. She needn't have bothered, since Greg was caught up in another conversation with a woman half his age, and the other people at the table were involved in some animated political discussion. "I never intended for it to be a social thing. Or anything else."

"Amy, you can't honestly tell me you no longer feel anything between us. Since we hugged at the restaurant, I haven't been able to stop thinking about you. I know I said we wouldn't have been good together, but I admit, I had kind of hoped, by moving to the area..."

Amy didn't bother to hide her incredulity. "Evelyn. There's no longer anything between us. I don't know if that's what you actually need to hear, but if it is, there you go. I don't want to date you. I don't really want anything to do with you, at all, ever again. Is that the clarity you need?" She wasn't trying to be mean, but the pieces were starting to click. Her presence in Amy's life wasn't coincidental.

"Because of Lena?"

"Because of me. Because we were over a long time ago, and it's time I figured that out and stop letting what you did mess up my life."

Evelyn stayed silent, clearly stunned. Amy walked back over to her table, feeling freer than she had in years.

"Where is Lena?"

Sarah shook her head. "I'm not sure. She just suddenly excused herself."

Amy knew where she would be. She headed over to the stairs and climbed the two flights to the observation deck. It was still overcast, not quite raining, but she figured Lena would look at the sky anyway.

She got to the top, cursing her heels. Lena was standing at the far end, holding the railing and looking up. There was an innocence to Lena that melted Amy's heart. She was sweet, sincere, kind, and generous. Amy hadn't known Lena's parents, but she'd bet they'd be incredibly proud of her.

"When did you start looking at them?"

Lena didn't turn around when she answered. "My dad kept his telescope at Lands End. We would look almost every night, from the time I could stand still long enough. It was my favorite thing to do."

Amy walked up beside her. "Which is your favorite?"

Lena didn't hesitate with her answer. "Gemini. They make the U shape, right over there." She pointed. "They represent the twins, Castor and Pollux. Only Pollux was immortal, and when his brother Castor was killed, he begged Zeus to give Castor immortality as well. So he did, by placing the brothers in the sky together."

"The original soul mates."

Lena smiled at her. "You read the book you gave me."

Amy stepped in front of her. She undid the button holding the jacket closed and ran her hands up Lena's sides. "I skimmed it."

Lena didn't make a move to stop her, so she continued. Lena was warm, and the way she slightly jumped when Amy put her hands on the side of her breasts made her heart speed up. "I'm sorry I had to leave you back there."

Lena put her arms around Amy and pulled her closer. "I don't want to talk about it right now."

There was an announcement made over the speaker system, informing the guests that fireworks would begin in ten minutes, and to start making their way to the observation deck. Lena leaned forward and kissed Amy's forehead, pulling her head into her chest. Amy liked this place in Lena's arms, where she felt safe and happy. Lena calmed her and excited her in a way no one ever had before. The contrast was wonderful. Amy wanted more. She looked up and saw those blue eyes staring back down at her. Tired of waiting, she pulled her head down and kissed her.

Each time kissing Lena was different. There was apprehension, passion, and excitement all rolled into one simple, silent action. Amy was in awe of how something so quiet and simple could say so much. Lena's mouth was so soft and tender. She took her time, lingering just long enough to excite Amy even more with each movement. The sounds of people coming up the stairs were not only annoying, they were frustrating. Lena softly kissed her two more times and then turned her around so she was facing toward the ocean. She wrapped her arms around her and pulled Amy against her body. Amy leaned her head back into Lena's chest and enjoyed the feel of her breathing rising and falling against her back. This was exactly where she wanted to be.

CHAPTER SIXTEEN

Ihad a really amazing time tonight. Thank you for inviting me." Lena looked over at Amy. The rain had finally started to come down, and the holiday lights that were still illuminated all over the city made the raindrops on the dark car window look like a kaleidoscope. They also highlighted the sweet, sultry beauty of Amy's face.

"Thank you for coming with me."

Lena watched Amy's hand travel up her arm. She didn't want the night to be over. She didn't want to stop touching Amy, or for Amy to stop touching her. She wanted her; she wanted all of her.

The car pulled up to Lena's house and they got out. Amy followed her to her front door and kissed her again. Her arms went around her neck, and Lena lost herself, and possibly found herself, in that very moment. "Come inside. Spend the night with me." Maybe she should have posed it as a question, but it wasn't one. She couldn't imagine wanting anything more.

Amy nodded, pulled off her heels, and ran back to the car to get her things and tell the driver to go. A few moments later, the car was driving off, and Amy was beside her again. Lena should have been nervous, but she wasn't. They walked inside, tossing their damp coats on the chair, the chair on which all coats lived.

Wordlessly, Lena took Amy's hand and led her upstairs. She quickly riffled through a drawer to find Amy something dry to wear and turned around with a T-shirt in hand.

Amy put a hand behind her back, unzipped her dress, and pushed it down. She stepped out of it and stood there, waiting. Lena knew she was staring, but she couldn't help it. Knee-weakening desire coursed through her, but she was rooted to the spot. Amy closed the distance between them. She reached back and unclasped her bra, letting it fall to the floor next to her dress. "I don't want to wear a T-shirt. I don't want to wear anything."

Lena wanted to speak, but she couldn't. All she could do was nod. Amy ran her hands up Lena's stomach, over her chest, and to her shoulders, pushing her jacket off. She slowly undid the tie, while she kept her green eyes focused on Lena's. She pulled the tie from around Lena's neck. "I don't want you to wear anything, either."

Lena nodded again. Amy undid each button on Lena's shirt. Lena looked down and watched her, but Amy wasn't as cool as she pretended to be, as her hands were slightly shaking. Somehow, that eased the slightly panicked feeling in Lena's chest, and she started to function again. Amy pushed the shirt off, leaned forward, and put her mouth against Lena's neck. "Put your hands on me."

Lena ran the tips of her fingers up Amy's sides and felt her shiver. Amy reached around her and unclasped her bra, dropping it on the floor before she took Lena's hand and walked her over to the bed, where she sat down. She put two fingers in the front of Lena's pants and pulled her over, so Lena was standing between her legs. She undid the two buttons and folded it open, then began to kiss Lena's stomach. She started at her bellybutton and slowed right where her underwear started as she slid her tongue along her skin, just above the material. Lena didn't understand how she was still standing. The only thing keeping her upright was the fear that if she moved, Amy would stop.

Amy pushed Lena's pants down and she stepped out of them. Together, they lay back on the bed, holding each other, their touches light, exploring. Lena's heart was racing, and she hoped her hands weren't shaking. She moved the hair off Amy's neck and used her fingers to trace a soft, light line down her chest and stomach. Amy's body twitched under the movement, and Lena continued her exploration, running her fingers down and then back up her left leg. Amy closed her eyes and bit her bottom lip. Lena watched in amazement as her expression became nothing but need. She rubbed the inside of her leg a little harder, and Amy's breath picked up.

She moved her hand slowly to between her legs, and a soft moan escaped Amy's throat. Lena rubbed with a little more intensity, eliciting another sound, this one filled with more need and a building fierceness. Lena moved her hand under Amy's underwear and pushed her fingers into the soft, warm wetness. Amy's hips shifted upward in response to Lena's movement, driving her own need even further. Lena leaned down and gave her a deep, long kiss. Amy's growing desire was multiplying with each stroke against her clit. Lena could feel it against her hand as Amy kissed her back. A few moments later, Amy pulled her mouth away as her breathing became more ragged, more desperate. She pushed her hips harder against Lena's hand, and then, clearly desperate, pulled Lena on top of her, biting down on her ear and then her neck. Lena felt Amy's breath hitch, and then, her fingers pressed hard against her back, she raked her teeth down Lena's shoulder and cried out underneath her as she arched into Lena's touch.

Lena knew the slightest movement against her was going to push her over the edge. Feeling Amy against her had driven her to a point of need she'd never experienced. Amy pushed her over on her back and climbed on top of her. Lena was trying to watch her, but her vision was hazy with need, her body desperate for release. Amy started at her collarbone, the excruciatingly slow pace maddening and exhilarating. She stopped at Lena's breasts and softly bit down on each one. Lena's hips twitched, and Amy pressed them back down, making it clear this was going to go at her pace. Knowing that made it even sexier. Amy moved down her body and lay between her legs. She ran her thumb down Lena's center, applying pressure just where it was needed. Lena gasped, her body apparently realizing it needed oxygen in order to sustain this. Then she felt Amy's mouth on her. It was the most amazing, sensual, vulnerable experience Lena could remember having. Amy's tongue moved slowly at first and then a bit faster. She reached up and held her hips in place, though Lena didn't realize she was moving them. The initial wave of euphoria raged through her like wildfire, reaching every part of her body. The next wave happened moments later and was unexpected. She didn't realize her body was trembling until Amy was lying beside her, kissing her cheek.

"That happened much faster than I was expecting." Lena felt like she could melt into the bed, her body was so relaxed. She kept her eyes closed, reveling in the feeling.

Amy continued to kiss her cheek. "Which part, the sex itself or the orgasm?"

Lena was still trying to catch her breath. "The second."

Amy softly bit Lena's jawline. "Let's go a bit slower this time, then."

"Oh, I'm not complaining. It hasn't ever happened to me."

Amy moved her mouth down Lena's neck. "Well, I'm all for breaking records."

Lena moved her head to give Amy access to the full length of her neck. Amy's purse started to ring. Lena thought it was Amy's purse, though it could have been her ears ringing from the dwindling blood flow to her head.

"Shit. I have to get that. It could be work."

Lena wanted to protest, but she said nothing. Maybe she'd just have to get used to Amy's job interrupting things.

Amy picked up her purse and pulled out her phone. She looked over at Lena. "I'm sorry." Then she answered, "This is Amy." She stood and walked across the room while she spoke. Lena took the brief moment to again appreciate how beautiful Amy really was. Her confidence in being naked was incredible. Lena silently hoped it was contagious.

"Yes, I understand. I'll be there in a bit." She hung up the phone and crawled back into bed.

"You have to go, don't you?" Lena said as Amy sprawled across her. She could see the tension in her eyes, even though she was clearly trying to hide it behind soft kisses.

"Yes, but I won't be long. I can come back, if you want."

Lena kissed the top of her head. "I do want. Very much."

Amy kissed her two more times and pushed herself out of bed. She pulled back on the discarded, wet clothing. She shivered as she adjusted it into place.

Lena moved the pillows to go under her head. "Do you want something to change into?"

Amy paused for a minute, seeming to think about it. "No, you're too tall and I can't go into the office in rolled sweatpants."

"My car keys are down on the table."

"Okay. I'm really sorry about this. I'll be back as soon as possible." She walked over and kissed Lena. The kiss quickly intensified from a simple good-bye to a heated exchange.

Lena thought about pulling her back into bed, but Amy's hand on her chest pushed her back.

"Don't lose that thought. I'll be right back." Amy kissed her again and then left.

Lena lay still until she heard the front door close. She briefly hoped Amy would change her mind and come back. When that didn't happen, she forced herself out of bed and into the bathroom. She turned the shower on, and while she waited for it to warm, she looked at herself in the mirror. Her skin was still flushed and red streaks marked her shoulders and back, sex trails from Amy's teeth and nails. A beautiful reminder of what had just happened between them. Lena smiled and stepped into the shower. It might have been sooner than she planned, but she had no regrets. It was time to let someone in.

❖

Amy maneuvered through the damp streets of San Francisco. Everything looked different; the air smelled different. She still had butterflies in her stomach, courtesy of the woman she had just left lying in a bed Amy could have stayed in forever. She could still smell a faint hint of Lena's perfume on her own body, and it evoked the feeling of Lena lying on top of her. All of her senses were on hyper alert, and Amy felt alive for the first time in a very long time. *Have I ever felt this way?* She grinned, enjoying the feeling, as well as the absence of anxiety that came with it.

She parked the car on the street and took a moment to compose herself. She needed to take care of this situation so she could go back to Lena. Sarah had sounded completely frazzled, and if it was bad enough to rattle her, it must be really bad. Sarah had just said it was an emergency, and she needed to get to Peter Reynolds's house right away. *I should have gotten at least a few details.* Amy didn't like walking into a potentially heated situation blindly. She got out of the car and pulled her jacket around a little tighter, walking up to the iron gate, unlocked and wide open. Amy walked through and started up the path. People were hurrying out, and then she saw one she recognized. It was like a punch in the stomach.

"Laura? What are you doing here?" Amy grabbed her arm and pulled her to the side. The young man she was with followed closely behind.

"Amy. Shit. It's not what you think." Laura held up her hands in a kind of surrender motion.

"Laura, you can't be anywhere near Peter Reynolds." Amy looked around for cameras, instantly on alert. *Lena is going to kill me.*

"I brought Ben here to meet him. We were talking about the Miners. I told him that I knew him, and he didn't believe me. I texted Peter, and he told me to come over for his party. I was only here for like, ten minutes."

The young man standing next to her kept nodding, as though to back her up. They both looked like scared kids, and Amy sighed. "Who is this?"

"This is Ben. He's Chloe's brother."

"Oh, this just keeps getting better and better."

"Amy, you can't tell my sister." Laura fell slightly to the side, Ben catching her elbow and rebalancing her.

Amy felt as if she were trapped in a very bad after-school special. "I have to tell your sister, Laura."

Laura shook her head. "No, you don't. We were here for ten minutes, fifteen minutes. I don't know; it wasn't long. Neither of us drank anything, did anything. Nothing happened. I just introduced him to Peter. We're leaving and going back to Ben's mom's house."

"You snuck out too?"

"She wouldn't have let us come." Laura's cheeks were flushed red, and her eyes were hazy.

Amy knew she needed to ask a question that she didn't want to know the answer to. "Laura, are you drunk?"

Laura looked at Ben, who was blatantly nervous, before answering. "No."

Amy knew she was lying. Now that she was focused on her, she could smell the slight hint of alcohol on her breath. "Ben, did she drink anything?"

"Oh my God. Fine. I had two, maybe three, drinks."

Ben finally spoke. "I didn't drink anything, and I'm going to get her back right now."

"Are you going to tell Lena? She'll ground me until I'm eighteen."

"You two have put me in a terrible spot here."

Ben, at least, looked like he felt guilty. Laura, on the other hand, looked panicked and defensive. Amy quickly took inventory. Laura was okay, Ben seemed completely sober, and they were on their way out the door. This could be figured out later. She needed to deal with the situation inside and get Laura and Ben off the property before anything showed up on social media.

Amy nodded. "I'll think about it. Now, please get out of here before someone takes a picture or before the cops are here to ask questions."

Laura hugged her, which was unexpected. She just hoped she was making the right decision. Laura and Ben disappeared down the street, and Amy continued her long trudge up the path and into the house. The music was still playing at a volume that was only acceptable to either the deaf or ridiculously intoxicated.

She searched the room for Peter, who was huddled over something on the floor. When she made it across the room, her fears were confirmed. A woman, probably in her early twenties, was curled in a fetal position, covered in vomit. Amy pushed two of the people standing over her out of the way. "What happened?"

Peter was mumbling, but she made out the word, "cocaine."

"Jesus, Peter! Did you call 911?"

Peter shook his head. "No, I called you."

"Oh my God." Amy pulled out her phone and dialed. She managed to find the wall plate that controlled the volume and turned the music all the way down. She described the situation and gave the address. She hung up the phone. "They're on their way." She leaned down and put her ear to the young woman's mouth while she felt for a pulse. It was there. Faint, but there. She was still breathing.

Amy had a million questions, but she needed to manage the situation and she needed to do it fast. "Peter, get upstairs and get in the shower. You're covered in vomit and there's blood on your shirt." He started to protest, but she gave him a pointed look and he headed upstairs. Amy glanced around the room for any signs of the illegal substance that the woman had ingested. She knew she didn't have much time for anything but a brief once-over. Fortunately, the situation and lack of music meant people started to wander off, so hopefully there wouldn't be so many around once the police and paparazzi showed up.

When she heard the sirens, Peter was still upstairs, and most of the people were gone, though there were still a few passed out on the couch and throughout the house. There was nothing she could do about that now.

Two men, gurney in tow, came through the front door. Amy motioned them over and watched as they did their initial assessment. Then they hoisted the woman on the gurney and put an oxygen mask over her face. They rushed her out the door and into the ambulance. The police unit that had showed up with the ambulance waited until it left, and then the officers walked up to Amy. She knew because of Good Samaritan laws, she wouldn't be in any type of trouble, or actually part of the investigation, but she was here to protect Peter. *Not that I should. Dumbass.*

She explained to the police officer that she had stopped by to see if Peter was home. He was apparently already in bed and the party was still going. She told them that was when she noticed the woman on the floor and called for help. She didn't know who she was, nor did the people who'd been around her. The police officer wrote everything down, along with her phone number. Amy knew they wouldn't push for more information, not at this address. Being wealthy and a professional athlete had its benefits. They asked to speak to Peter, and she told them he was passed out in bed, dead to the world.

The whole process took about thirty minutes from the time she walked through the door until the police car pulled away from the house. She walked back in and sat on the couch, ignoring the random people passed out through the living room. She pulled out her phone and flipped through her contacts, finding the phone number for Peter's lawyer. She went back through the scenario with him and avoided making the obvious comment that this was the third time they'd had a similar discussion on New Year's.

The lawyer said he would send someone down to the hospital to take care of any medical bills and confidentiality disclosures. Amy hung up and closed her eyes. *When did I become a babysitter for asshats?*

Peter came down the stairs, talking on the phone. He hung up and pointed to indicate who was on the other end. "My agent. I had to warn him so he can deal with the team. I'm on some bullshit probation for behavior."

"I thought you were out of town." Amy was too tired and disgusted for pleasantries.

"I'm on the bench. Blew out my knee."

"Where's your wife?"

"Vegas."

Amy nodded and got up. "You need to call your lawyer in the morning. I've already started the ball rolling."

"What's going to happen?"

"Don't you mean, 'is that woman going to be okay?'" Amy shouldn't be losing her patience. Peter Reynolds was an extension of her biggest client. She couldn't afford to make him angry. But at the moment, she just didn't care anymore.

"She was still breathing. She'll be fine."

Amy was appalled. Not just with him, but with herself too. "I don't know who had pictures of tonight, or who will leak this to the press. Is there anything I should know?"

Peter poured what she assumed was whiskey into a glass and drank it down in one gulp. "There were some girls here tonight. We spent some…uh…time together."

Amy felt an invisible hand clutch her stomach and throat. *Please not Laura.* "How old?"

"College girls, from Stanford. I had Mike check their IDs."

Amy felt the slightest bit of relief. "Are they still here?"

He pointed up the stairs. "Passed out."

Amy walked to the door. "Call me tomorrow if you need me." There was more she could have done. This had the potential to be a media circus if there were pictures, video, Snapchats, Periscopes, live feeds, one of any number of other social media nightmares. Part of her also hoped it did get out, and he was ruined. Not something her partners would be happy to discover, but it meant she wouldn't have to deal with his absurd, juvenile behavior anymore.

She walked out the front door and down the path to Lena's car. She was angry, and that anger confused her. She told herself she just needed to get out of there, that she would feel better in the morning. Everything always looked a bit brighter in the morning. *It is morning. And a hell of a start to the new year.*

She climbed the stairs to Lena's bedroom, trying to be quiet. The last time she made this trip, it was with an entirely different sense of urgency. Amy needed to shower, sleep, lie next to Lena, and try to put things in perspective. She started the same process of pulling her clothes off as she did the last time, and she headed for the shower. Lena was sound asleep, and didn't so much as stir as Amy walked past her on the way to the bathroom.

Amy smelled her dress. She knew it didn't actually smell like vomit, since she hadn't gotten any on her, but she couldn't convince herself. She balled it up and put it in the little trash bin before she stepped into the shower and let the hot water sluice over her. It didn't matter how long she stood here for, a shower wasn't going to wash away what she was feeling, no matter how hard she scrubbed.

Amy climbed back into Lena's bed, unsure where, specifically, she should lie. She stared at the ceiling, her mind whirling. Lena stirred and rolled over, draping her arm around Amy. She caught a faint whiff of Lena's soap mixed in with her natural smell, and the storm in her mind calmed. Lena was everything that was good in the world. To Amy, she represented goodness, generosity, and an incredible sense of optimism. Amy aimlessly ran her fingertips up and down Lena's arm.

"Everything okay?"

Her voice was heavy, caught somewhere between a dream state and the here and now. Amy wasn't going to wake her just to fill her mind with the chaos and ugliness she had just helped disarm. Ugliness her little sister had apparently witnessed, and participated in. So she said nothing, and a few moments later, Lena's breathing became rhythmic as she slipped back to sleep.

What am I going to do? If she told Lena, she might freak out and decide she didn't want to see Amy anymore, because it was Amy's world Laura was messed up in. A world she had helped to steady, once again. Then again, if she didn't tell Lena, and she found out, she'd be pissed off that Amy lied to her. She wasn't overly concerned with Laura's reaction either way, since she was a teenager and she'd get over it. *It might actually be good for her to get caught.* She was flirting with dangerous behavior. But the thought of losing Lena made her feel sick, and she wasn't sure if she could take the chance. She kissed Lena's shoulder, feeling as though the world had suddenly become very fragile.

CHAPTER SEVENTEEN

L ena stared at the eggs in the frying pan. She was hoping she could somehow harness the hereditary ability to create edible food out of a raw mess her mother had managed to perfect. She heard the front door open and close again as familiar voices traveled into the kitchen.

"Hey."

Lena looked over at her sister and Chloe. "Hey. Good morning." She moved the heap of yellow and white around in the pan.

"What in the world are you trying to do?" Laura walked over and looked in the pan. "How do you mess up eggs?"

Lena shook her head and shrugged. "I honestly have no idea. I thought this would be one thing I couldn't mess up."

Laura took the spatula from her. "Well, you thought wrong. Move." Laura started moving the little mounds around with efficiency and a proficiency Lena had never noticed before. "Do you have vegetables to put in here, or is this your end game?"

Lena opened the fridge and pulled out onions and mushrooms and held them up to her like a treasure she had just discovered.

"Can you cut them up? You do know how a knife works, right?"

Lena walked over to the island and pulled out the cutting board and knife. "I guess my hope that you would abandon sarcasm as a New Year's resolution was just wishful thinking, huh?"

Chloe walked over and grabbed the mushrooms, taking them to the sink to wash. "Here, I'll help."

Lena could tell Chloe had questions she wanted answered immediately, because that's just how Chloe worked. She wasn't going to ask them in front of Laura though, no matter how much the curiosity was splitting her head.

"How was your night?" Lena cut the onions as she tossed the question at Laura.

"Good, fine, nothing exciting. You?" Laura dropped bread into the toaster without turning around.

Usually, Laura would have given her attitude, stating it was "whatever" and using a sigh as an exclamation point. This answer came out a little too chipper and a little too quick. "Do anything fun?"

"Just ate dinner and watched movies. Went to bed early."

Chloe had finished chopping the mushrooms as Lena finished the onions. They dropped them into the eggs.

Laura looked irritated. "You should have sautéed those first."

Lena crossed her arms and leaned against the counter closest to her. She noticed the distinct lack of eye contact. She looked over at Chloe, who simply shrugged.

"Morning." Amy's voice was tentative and still slightly cracked from sleeping.

Lena moved away from the counter and filled a coffee cup for her. Chloe and Laura both looked at Lena for a moment. She just gave them a small smile and went back to cooking.

Chloe grabbed a cup out of the same cabinet. "I'm going to need coffee."

The awkward silence was becoming a bit overwhelming. Lena decided to break it up and just say what everyone was thinking. "Yes, Amy spent the night."

Chloe sipped her coffee. "You don't say."

Laura put the food on plates and had even managed to cut up fruit, apparently while Lena wasn't paying attention. She set them in front of everyone and started toward the stairs. "I'm going to go take a shower."

Lena watched her disappear, still thrown by her odd behavior. She looked over at Chloe, who simply shook her head.

"Don't look at me. I don't speak Laura any better than you."

Amy pointed at her plate with her fork. "This is really good. The kid can cook."

Lena took a bite and her eyes widened. "There's feta cheese in here. I didn't even know we had feta cheese."

Chloe had a ridiculous grin on her face. "So...what did you two do last night?"

Amy practically choked on her eggs. "Can you two at least wait until I'm gone?"

Lena ignored Chloe's questions and looked at Amy. "What are your plans for the day?"

"I have to go into the office and deal with the situation from last night. I'm hoping it won't take long."

"Oh, okay." Lena sipped her coffee.

"Lena doesn't have plans. Well, she did have plans, but now she doesn't. Lena, I'm cancelling our plans. You're free."

Lena rolled her eyes. "Do you want to get together after you're done?"

Amy put her hand over Lena's. "I'd like that." She smiled at Chloe. "Thank you." She finished the last few bites and took her plate over to the sink. "I have to get going. I already called for a car to take me home." She looked down at the oversized pajamas she had thrown on. "Can I bring these back to you later?"

Lena walked over to the sink and pulled Amy close. "Yes, of course you can. Is it okay if we meet here?"

Amy hugged Lena, holding her for longer than Lena expected, but it was welcomed. "Sure. I'll call when I'm on my way." She let go and walked past Chloe. "Bye, Chloe."

A few moments later, the door shut and Chloe smacked her in the arm. "Tell me EVERYTHING."

Lena couldn't control the smile that made her cheekbones hurt. She grabbed the coffee pot and took a seat on the bar stool next to Chloe.

❖

Amy pinched the bridge of her nose. She had spent the last six hours poring over every piece of social media she could find that could potentially have exposed Peter Reynolds. She had found a few pictures from the party, but there was nothing incriminating. And thankfully, she hadn't seen anything with Laura in it. *Small mercies.* She had thought about calling Sarah in, but then thought better of it. Super Sarah could enjoy her day off. *Someone should be able to.*

Amy moved her head back and forth, trying to loosen up the muscles in her neck. Her phone vibrated on the desk and she grabbed it like a lifeline. Disappointingly, it wasn't Lena. "Hey, Brit."

"Hey, Amy. Have you spoken with Lena?"

"Not since this morning, why?" Amy put her elbows on her desk.

"The article came out today and I haven't heard from her. I was just wondering what she thought."

Amy closed her eyes, disappointed with herself that she'd forgotten. Today was probably a very hard day for Lena and her sister, and it hadn't even crossed her mind because she'd been so caught up with Peter Reynolds. "No, I haven't. I'm going to see her tonight."

"Okay, well, she doesn't owe me a check-in or anything. I was just curious."

Amy couldn't even offer any feedback or encouragement. As usual, her job was all-consuming, and she certainly hadn't had time to read the paper. "Sorry, Brit. I'm sure it's great."

"Okay, if she wants to talk about it, have her call me."

"Will do. Bye."

Amy pulled up the article on her computer. Each sentence made her feel a bit closer to Lena. Brittany had done a great job of portraying the sisters, while still keeping certain aspects private. When she reached the part where Laura recounted the events from that evening, Amy's heart broke for the little girl who was forever changed that night.

It was seven years ago, but I still remember it as if it happened last night. It was rainy and cold. Usually, my dad stayed at home with me, but that night he had to take me in because the night manager had gotten sick. I was supposed to be lying down in the office, but I had gone to the big window at the side of the restaurant so I could watch the lightning hit the bay. I heard my dad arguing with someone out front, so I went out to see what was happening.

There was a man standing at the hostess desk. He had a gun pointed at my parents and was yelling at them to give him the money from the night deposit. He kept yelling it was owed to him. I remember watching the water that had gathered on his jacket. It kept falling to the ground, and it reminded me of a dog shaking off his coat after getting out of the water. It's funny how you picture things when you're little. Anyway, my mom saw me and started to cry. That must have been when he realized I was there, because he yelled at me to come to the front with my parents. I still don't know why I listened. I guess because I was scared and wanted to be with them. Looking back, if I had made him come after me, maybe things would have turned out differently. I'll always regret doing what I was told that night.

My mom yelled at me to stay back, and it just made him angrier. He pushed the gun toward her face and told me to hurry up, so I did. My mom was gripping my shoulders so hard it hurt. I tried to look at his face, but I could only make out portions because of the hood that covered part of his face. All I knew for sure was that he was white and had a scar on his chin that stretched down to his throat.

My dad kept telling him that he had given him all the money and there was nothing left in the restaurant, but the man kept yelling for more. My dad took off his watch and gave him his wallet. When the first shot went off, I thought it was the lightning. It was so loud and bright. Then my dad fell down, and I thought he had lost his balance or had been scared by the lightning, too. My mom screamed, and it made me jump. Her scream was cut off, though, because there was another shot, another burst of lightning. But I had been wrong both times; it wasn't lightning at all. I leaned over and tried to shake my mom. I remember yelling for her to wake up, but every time I pushed her body, nothing happened. But there was blood. So much blood, and I remember how warm it was, and how that scared me more than anything. I heard the last gunshot, although I don't remember feeling anything.

I woke up in the hospital. My older sister, Lena, was there, and she told me I'd been shot too. I remember thinking that the pain in my side, where the bullet had entered, should have hurt more, but it didn't. All I felt was the agony of my parents being gone. I've felt that loss every day since.

Amy didn't realize she was crying until a teardrop fell on the keyboard. She hurt for a little girl she had never known, and for the young woman she had become. For the first time since meeting them, the gravity of what the Michaels sisters had endured really hit her. It covered her like a wet, cold blanket.

She grabbed her coat off the back of the chair and headed for her car.

❖

Lena sat on her couch, staring at the tree of life that hung in her living room. It had been there her whole life, but she never tired of looking at it. She sipped her red wine and listened to the rain hit the window that covered the wall behind her. Laura was up in her room, where she had been the majority of the day. The article had been difficult for them both to read. Not because it wasn't true or painted them in a light they didn't like, but because reliving it was hard. Lena hoped she had made the right decision, letting Laura participate in the interview.

There was a knock at the front door, and she suspected it was Chloe coming by to check on them. "Come in."

Amy walked into the living room moments later. Her cheeks were red from the cold and her hair and clothes were damp from the rain. She looked beautiful. "Are you okay?"

Lena was both surprised and relieved to see her. "Yes. I'm fine." She paused. "I think I'm fine. My experience was so different from Laura's. I had to deal with the aftermath, but she actually had to live through it. I have tried a thousand times to try to put myself in her shoes, but I just can't. I don't think anyone could."

Amy sat down next to her. She put her hand on Lena's leg and rubbed it in a soothing motion. "It's okay not to be okay, Lena. It's okay to feel the loss again, and it's okay to feel a bit helpless."

Lena took her hand and nodded her agreement. "I'm more worried about Laura. She's been in her room since she read the article." Amy nodded and Lena continued. "I just hope I did the right thing. It has been years since she's had to go through the motions of that night again. I don't know, maybe I should get her back into counseling."

"I don't think that's true."

"What do you mean?"

"I think Laura probably replays that night, every day."

The thought sat on Lena, constricted her breathing, and she felt like someone was squeezing her lungs. She'd thought Laura had moved on, the way she had. "Yes, you're probably right."

"I know it's not my place to say anything, but maybe letting her be alone isn't what's best for her right now."

Lena sipped her wine. "I tried talking to her, but she doesn't want to talk."

Amy looked hesitant for a moment. "Do you mind if I try?"

Lena thought about it. She didn't mind, and the offer made her like Amy more. "You can try, but don't be surprised if she shuts you out."

Amy took off her coat and went up the stairs.

"It's the door at the end of the hall." Lena closed her eyes, drained and unsure what to do next. The fact that she had someone in the house willing to take even a little bit off her shoulders was an exceptionally comforting surprise. She could really learn to like not being alone.

Amy stared at the white door, suddenly feeling awkward. She wasn't entirely certain what made her offer to talk to Laura. She didn't know her, they had never had a real conversation, and Laura was asking her to keep a secret from Lena. But for some reason, that secret made her feel as if they had a connection. She tapped on the door twice. "Laura?"

"Amy?"

"Can I come in?"

"Yeah, I guess."

Amy pushed the door open and stepped inside. The walls were covered in posters, the typical array of teenage wishes, including photos of boys from a variety of bands in different stages of shenanigans pinned to the walls. There was also a UC

Davis flag that hung in the corner, which Amy noted showed her adoration for her sister and possibly her desire to be like her. "How are you doing?" Laura was lying on her bed and hadn't put down her phone.

"Fine. Why?"

Amy sat in the chair at the desk. She reminded herself that talking to people in various stages of distress was what she did best. "Well, I know I wouldn't be, so I wanted to see if you were."

Laura continued to play on her phone, but she didn't ask Amy to leave. "It's whatever."

Amy was going to need a different approach. "Those eggs were amazing this morning. I know you didn't learn that from your sister."

The statement actually made Laura chuckle. "Yeah, no kidding."

"Have you always liked to cook?"

Laura finally looked up from her phone. "Yeah, but I don't do it for Lena often."

"Why? If I were her, I would have you cooking every night."

She shrugged. "I don't like to upset her."

It was starting to come into focus. "Is that why you're up here? You don't want to upset Lena?"

Laura put her phone down and sat up, hugging her knees to her chest. "I found one of my mom's old recipe books a while back and just started trying different things. I don't know how Lena would feel about it."

"I bet she'd be pretty happy that someone in this house could prepare edible food."

Laura's smile was sad. "She misses them. I mean, I do too, but it's harder for her." She stared at the wall, clearly not looking at what was there. "She had to give up everything when they died, to come home and take care of me."

"Do you really think she would have wanted anything different?"

"No, I mean I know she wouldn't have wanted me to go into foster care or anything. But she had to give it all up, and I get to leave here in a few years and go do what I really want. Lena never wanted to run that restaurant."

"I see. So you think she resents you."

Laura picked at her comforter. "I don't know, but I think when she reads about what happened she thinks the same thing that I do. It could have gone differently if I had just done something."

"Laura, you were nine years old. There was nothing you could have done. I haven't spoken to Lena about it, but I know she doesn't blame you for any of it."

"I know she doesn't blame me, but sometimes I wonder if she wishes I had…you know. So she could have her life back."

Amy wanted to go over to the bed and hug her. So much pain, confusion, and despair clung to her young soul. But she wasn't sure if Laura would be okay with someone in her personal space when she was feeling so vulnerable. "Oh, Laura, Lena loves you. She would do anything for you. Everything she does, every time she gets mad at you, grounds you, yells at you, it's because she loves you. This may have not been what she had pictured, but it's how things worked out, and I know she wouldn't trade you for anything."

"I don't know."

"Ha! You should have seen her the first day she came into my office. I've never dealt with anyone so hell-bent on protecting a loved one. You hit the jackpot with sisters, kid."

Laura was trying to hide the fact that she was tearing up. She leaned back in her bed and picked up her phone again. "Thanks, Amy."

Amy stood to go. "You should come downstairs. Maybe we can all play a game or something. You know, it would be better if you could help each other through these times, rather than trying to do it without each other. It's good to lean on your sister. You never know, she might need your support too."

"Yeah, maybe."

Amy started to walk out, hoping she'd managed to help in some way.

"Oh and, Amy, thanks for not telling her about last night."

Amy's heart clenched. She still wasn't sure if she was making the right decision. She took a deep breath and reminded herself nothing bad had happened and Laura was okay. "I won't do it again, Laura."

Lena finished washing the coffee cups that had been filled with hot chocolate. She listened to Laura and Amy laugh in the background, saying good night to each other. It had been the best evening she'd had in a long time with Laura. They had played board games for hours. The laughter and joy that filled the room warmed a place in Lena's heart that had never been awoken until tonight. It had felt like…family. Her own, though, not someone else's. She heard her sister climb the stairs, and moments later, the door shut. It didn't slam; there was no yelling; it simply shut. It was a beautiful sound.

She felt Amy's arms come around her and she turned around in the embrace. "I don't know what you said to her, but thank you."

Amy continued to hug her. "I don't know how to duplicate it, so don't ask. Just enjoy it while it lasts."

Lena laughed. "Fair enough."

She tilted Amy's face up and leaned down and kissed her. Amy wrapped her arms around Lena's neck and pulled her closer. Lena didn't know how it was possible, but every time she kissed Amy, she felt it in every part of her body. Her fingers tingled, her chest warmed, her senses were on fire.

Lena took Amy's hand and walked her up the stairs. They walked into her room, and Lena closed the door, locking it behind them.

"Expecting me to stay?"

Lena knew Amy was trying to make a joke, but she didn't have enough wits about her to participate in the joshing banter. Instead, she slid her hands under Amy's shirt. With the slightest touch, she ran her fingertips up and down Amy's sides. Amy went to take off her shirt, and Lena stopped her. "We're going to take our time tonight."

Lena kissed her again, drawing each moment out, inciting a bit more passion each time she moved her mouth against Amy's. Lena moved her mouth to Amy's ear and down her neck. She felt Amy shiver beneath her lips and couldn't help but smile. They walked over to the bed, and Lena continued to brush Amy's skin, leaving a trail of goose bumps with each pass.

Amy's breathing continued to change, becoming more rapid as Lena bit on the bottom of her ear. She sat up and pulled her shirt over the top of her head, tossing it to the ground. Amy's eyes were heavy, hazy looking. Lena slid up Amy's shirt and kissed her stomach, moved up her sides and then back down. Amy put her hands in Lena's hair, as though she needed to hang on, to touch her without stopping the other sensations. Lena reached the top of her stomach below her bra and lightly raked her teeth over the sensitive skin.

Amy pulled off her shirt and unhooked her bra, tossing them to the floor. Lena continued her exploration of Amy as she lay back down, taking the time neither of them seemed to have patience for the night before. Amy's body began to writhe under Lena's touch as she moved her mouth over Amy's breasts. Lena bit down slightly, and hearing Amy whimper with pleasure excited her more than she could have anticipated.

Lena moved back down her body until she reached her pants. She unbuttoned the jeans and pulled them off, her underwear following quickly behind, leaving Amy naked and exposed. Lena was overwhelmed once again by her beauty. Her skin ran hot, which turned to scorching as she ran her hand up and down her legs. She lay down next to Amy and kissed her. Amy's need was becoming more apparent as she bit down on Lena's lip. She didn't stop Amy when she removed her pants, and seeing the look of lust in Amy's eyes as she looked her over made her feel sexier than she ever had before.

When Lena reached Amy's warm, slick heat, Amy moaned and pulled her closer. Lena was consumed by the touch and by Amy's body throbbing against her. Her enthrallment heightened as Amy's hand moved down against her as well, crippling any awareness she was clinging to as she sank into her. Lena felt the pulsing start, filling up inside her, threatening to explode at any moment. She continued to move her hand against Amy, felt the muscles around her fingers starting to clench. Amy bit down on Lena's shoulder to muffle her cry of ecstasy. Amy's breath on her shoulder and neck, the sounds escaping her throat, were in sync with what was happening inside Lena as well. The first cry Amy let out sent Lena over the edge, but this time, she wasn't afraid of landing. It flashed through her whole body, dragging its proverbial nails across every nerve ending in Lena's body.

They lay there a few moments later, wrapped up in each other. A light sheen of sweat caused their skin to cling together. Lena caught the last few kisses against her shoulder before she slipped into a heavy, contented sleep.

Chapter Eighteen

Lena sat in the busy room, watching the buzz all around her while waiting for Matt to get off the phone. Police officers moved in all different directions. Some were holding files, some were on phones, while others had people in handcuffs in tow. This was the ninth time in the several weeks since the article she'd been asked to come to the station to talk about a possible lead. Matt hung up and looked at her thoughtfully.

"How have you been?"

Lena nodded. "Good. Great, actually. You know that though. We had dinner with you three days ago. What's going on?"

Matt slid a folder in front of her. "I think this time the lead is actually legit."

Lena opened the inconspicuous manila folder. It was just a formality. She never really knew what she was looking at on these pages. "Another tip?"

Matt leaned closer to her. "This tip actually holds some weight. But I wanted to warn you about it first."

Lena stared at him, hoping she wouldn't have to draw each sentence out of him. "Matt, what's going on?"

Matt nodded at the file. "Look."

She looked down at the picture paper-clipped to the first page of the file. Her breath caught in her chest. Her ears grew hot and she felt a little dizzy. The photo staring back at her was of a man with a scar that ran from his chin to his throat. She took a deep breath to steady herself. "Where did this information come from?"

"Before I answer that, do you think Laura would be able to identify him? I know you didn't want to drag her in here each time we came upon a possibility."

Lena kept staring at the photo. "I don't know. She was only nine. Matt, where did you find him?"

Matt still looked like he didn't want to tell her, but he continued anyway. "From your dad's brother."

The room spun and Lena held onto the desk edge. "I'm sorry. What?"

"Lena, I know this isn't easy for you to hear, but the person with the tip claims to be your uncle. All he would give us was the name. He won't tell us any more until he talks to you."

There was a throbbing in Lena's head. Every tiny sound seemed more pronounced. She heard a coffee cup being set down on a desk, a stapler in the background. "That's ridiculous. Make him talk to you."

"It doesn't exactly work like that. There was no way he could have been part of the crime because he was serving time in San Quentin when it happened. Right now, all we have is a working theory."

"I don't know where to find him."

"Well, he's here."

Lena couldn't breathe. She leaned forward, tempted to actually put her head between her legs. The information was overwhelming. She put her shaking hand on his desk. "I don't know if I can see him."

Matt put his hand on top of hers. "I can go in with you, if you want."

Suddenly feeling claustrophobic, she stood up. "I need some air." She walked out of the busy room and straight out of the building. The late February air felt good on her skin. She looked around for a place to go, anywhere, but the station was alone in the area, set apart from its surroundings by large fields of grass. The cool breeze calmed her need to run and relieved the feeling of wanting to faint. She sat on a concrete bench, a million different things running through her mind. Questions that could only be answered by one person, and he was sitting inside a police station, ten feet away.

She thought briefly of calling Amy, then of Chloe, and finally, Laura. She owed it to her to go confront this man that claimed to be her uncle. She owed it to her parents to bring their potential killer to justice, if, in fact, he really knew what had happened. She owed it to herself. She looked back up at the front door of the station. Matt was standing outside, apparently waiting for her. *Or he's making sure I don't run.*

She turned her face to the breeze again, took a deep breath, and walked back toward the doors that, once she walked through them, would change her life forever. She reached the place where Matt was standing. "Okay, I'll talk to him."

Matt nodded and pulled the door open. "You're making the right decision."

Lena nodded. "We'll see."

They walked back through the busy room and down a hallway. They finally reached a room labeled "Conference Room 1." The glass wall allowed Lena to look at the man who sat on the other side. He had a scruffy brown beard, streaked with gray. His hair looked dirty, and there were dark circles under his eyes. He had blue eyes, identical to her father's. Lena's stomach turned. She didn't think it was possible. She pushed the door open and walked in and took a seat at the large table.

"You look just like her. I mean, I saw the pictures in the paper, but in person it's even more incredible."

Lena didn't know what she was expecting, but someone commenting on her resemblance to her mother wasn't it. "What do you want?"

"I want to make things right."

Lena couldn't believe what she was hearing. "Make what right? I've never even met you. I don't know who you are, or why you're here, but apparently, you've got information about what happened to my family. What do you want?"

His voice stayed calm, in spite of Lena's raising volume level. "I thought you and your sister deserved an explanation."

At the mention of Laura, Lena became even more agitated. "You aren't going anywhere near Laura."

He put his hands up, as if he were surrendering. "I understand. I just want to talk."

Lena leaned back in her chair and rolled her eyes, motioning for him to continue. She needed this over quickly, before she fell apart.

"How much do you know about your dad's side of the family?"

"Almost nothing. For example, I don't even know your name."

"I'm Nathan."

Lena stared at him, waiting for him to continue.

"Your dad was my older brother. Our dad, well…he was a drunk. A very abusive, very mean drunk. So mean that our mom took off when we were kids."

Lena wasn't sure what to believe. "She just left you all with him?"

He nodded. "I don't blame her, not anymore, anyway. She was fifteen when she had your dad, seventeen when she had me, gone by nineteen. What do you really know at nineteen? Anyway, I'll spare you the details, but let's just say it fell on your dad to take care of me."

That sounded like her father. He was a caring, compassionate man. What didn't make sense was how Nathan had ended up being what he was. Her father wasn't one to give up on someone.

"I got hooked on meth when I was very young. Your dad was in college at the time. He did what he could, but I disappeared for a while. He eventually found me and moved me in with your mom and him."

Nathan leaned back in his seat. His shirt was full of holes, and it was the first time she noticed the strong stench coming from his body. Lena fought her almost natural instinct of concern. "Okay, keep going."

"Well, I couldn't kick the habit. Your mom got pregnant with you. Your dad put me into rehab, but I didn't want to be there. As soon as I got out, I went right back to doing what I had always been doing. I tried coming by a few times, but never actually knocked on the door. Your dad was right. I had no business being around a kid." He looked down at his hands as he rubbed them together, with more force than was necessary. "He would find me on the streets, bring me food and blankets. He kept offering to pay for me to go back to rehab, but I didn't want to go. This went on for years." He looked up at Lena. "He never gave up, ya know." He looked back down. "Anyway, meth ain't cheap, and I got pinched for a robbery I had pulled off with a buddy, where someone got hurt real bad. I only got out a few weeks ago. I didn't even know anything had happened to your parents. I just figured they didn't know what happened, and your dad had finally given up on me. I was too ashamed to write and tell your dad where I was."

"Then how do you know anything about who killed them?"

He coughed and wiped tears out of his eyes. "I had gotten my dealer to give me an advance, telling him my brother owned a restaurant, and he'd lend me the money to pay for it. I had been going to him for years, so he did me a favor. I guess when he found out I was in jail, he went to collect."

Rage, pure and red, pulsed through her. But what came out of her mouth was eerily calm. The moment was surreal. "My parents were killed for *your* IOU on drugs?"

He nodded, looking completely defeated. "I'm afraid so. When I read the description of the guy your sister gave, in that news article, I knew it was him."

"Do you have any idea what you've done to my sister and me?"

"I know it doesn't help, but I'm sorry."

"It doesn't help."

"I'm trying to make it right." He rubbed his arms. "I'm sober now."

He looked up at Lena with those blue eyes. Her father's eyes. "I don't care."

"I don't deserve your forgiveness. I just wanted to do the right thing."

Lena stood up, the chair scraping the hard floor. "Stay away from us."

He nodded. "I will. I'm sorry. I'm so, so sorry."

Lena pulled the door open and heard him say softly, "Your father never loved anything as much as he loved you."

She walked out without acknowledging him. Matt was standing outside, waiting. "He's all yours."

Amy placed her cell phone on her desk after the call ended and turned to stare at the Pacific Ocean, hoping it would magically wash away what she was feeling. She heard the footsteps behind her.

"Matt told me what happened."

Amy turned around to look at Sarah, who looked genuinely concerned. "Yeah, I just got off the phone with Lena."

"This is a good thing though, right?"

Amy shook her head. She really wasn't sure what kind of "thing" this was at all. "I think in the long run it will be, but right now it's just a lot for them to take in. They found out what happened to their parents, while discovering they have a drug-addicted uncle that was the underlying cause of the whole thing." She felt the heaviness of the information and hurt the girls must be feeling. "I don't know."

Sarah sat on the corner of Amy's desk. "Is there anything I can do?"

Amy tapped her leg and smiled at her. "No, you're very sweet for offering, though."

"Are you going over there?"

"No, Lena wants time with her sister." Amy wanted nothing more than to rush over and be with them, but Lena had said she needed time with Laura to make sure she was okay. She was worried about Lena and Laura, but more than that, she was hurting for them and wanted to be there to offer her support. In the two months they'd been seeing each other, their lives had become more intertwined than Amy had been with anyone since Evelyn.

Amy forced herself not to take it personally. Lena not wanting her there had nothing to do with her; the pain from this ran long and deep. If Lena needed her, she would let her know. The Michaels girls needed space right now, and Amy wanted to do whatever they needed. "Want to go get a drink?"

Sarah stood up and went for her coat. "Thought you would never ask."

By the time they'd had a few drinks and Amy had gotten ready for bed, she still hadn't heard from Lena. It was rare they spent a night apart these days, and the bed felt enormous without her. *Everything is okay. She'll call tomorrow.* She tried to quell the fear and insecurity as she drifted into an uneasy sleep.

CHAPTER NINETEEN

Lena checked her cell phone for the hundredth time in the last twenty minutes. Chloe reached over and pushed the phone down.

"Lena, I know you're worried. I'm worried. But we're going to find her."

Lena stood up and started pacing. "I don't know where the hell she could have gone. I called Marcy. I called Katie. I even called Julie, and I'm pretty sure she doesn't like Julie anymore. None of them have heard from her."

Chloe walked over to the sink and filled a glass with water. She handed it to Lena, who took a sip and continued her pacing. "Have you heard back from Ben yet?"

Chloe shook her head. "Not yet."

Lena practically collapsed on the couch, and then stood immediately back up. "We need to be looking for her. We need to get out of here."

"No, my parents are driving around everywhere. We need to stay here in case she comes home."

Lena ran her hands through her hair, as though trying to hold her head in place. "Thirty more minutes and I'm calling the police."

The door opened and Amy walked in. She walked up to Lena and hugged her. She took a step back and kept her hands on her arms. "Are you okay?"

As soon as she saw Amy, she wanted to break down. Amy made her emotions more raw, she made her feel more vulnerable, but somehow more supported, too. Lena felt like she could fall apart with Amy there. "I don't know where she is. I don't even know how long she's been gone." She let some tears fall and leaned into her embrace.

Amy stroked her back and whispered, "We're going to find her."

Lena squeezed Amy tighter, needing the closeness. Amy grounded her when nothing else could.

"I'm going to look through her room again and see if I missed anything."

Lena ran up the stairs as fast as her legs would carry her. *There has to be something. Please let me find something.*

❖

"What do we know?"

Chloe curled up on the couch. "Lena said they talked most of the night, and then she got up this morning and Laura was gone."

Amy felt sick to her stomach. The worst possible scenarios were racing through her head. There were a million possible explanations and only a few possible outcomes. Only one of those outcomes was acceptable. Laura needed to make it home in one piece.

Amy looked down at her phone and scrolled to the name she didn't want to call. Peter Reynolds. If Laura was with him, she could get her home, but that also meant she was with him, and that brought a whole host of other issues.

Lena came down the stairs, frantic. "That's it. I'm calling the cops."

Amy felt a burning sensation run down the back of her throat. If the cops were called and Laura was with Peter, there was no amount of media control she could do to prevent that nightmare. A professional football player harboring an underage runaway wasn't something she wanted to deal with. She hated herself for even thinking it. Considering Peter and his despicable, piecemealed reputation meant nothing in the face of finding Laura.

"Let me try one place first. Don't call the cops." She said it without thinking.

Lena looked at her, confused. "Where are you thinking?"

Amy wished she had just made the phone call, but it was too late. "I'm going to try Peter Reynolds." She walked out the door before she had a chance to see Lena's expression.

She hung up the phone with no more information than she had started with. She turned around to see Lena standing directly behind her.

"Why in the hell would Peter Reynolds know where my sister was?"

Amy didn't want to lie, not to Lena, not when she was scared and things were already so crazy. "Because he saw her after Christmas, and I thought maybe they were still in contact."

The look on Lena's face hurt more than if she had just hit her. "How do you know that?"

Amy felt the tears coming, but she pushed them away, wanting to stay strong. "I saw her at his house on New Year's Eve. That phone call I got was to go to his house because of a problem at his party. She'd had a few drinks, but Ben was taking her home—"

Lena's eyes got bigger. Normally, when Amy looked into them she saw calmness, peace, her safe place. That had been replaced with betrayal and anger.

"You need to go."

Amy tried to grab her, to make her understand. "Lena, please."

Lena moved away from Amy's attempt to grab her arm. "It's bad enough you lied to me. Then you try to put off me calling the police for my missing sister. For what? To protect his image? Where is your line, Amy? I thought I knew you."

Amy started to cry. "Lena, it wasn't like that. I mean, yes, I thought about that for a second, but Laura is more important. *You* are more important. I called him to make sure Laura wasn't with him. If we call the police, and she's with him, she'll end up in the media circus that surrounds that bastard. I just thought if we could get her back without a public scene—"

"Get off my property." Lena crossed her arms. Her eyes were still on fire; fury and passion burned in that ice blue.

Amy could barely breathe. She was trying to get herself under control, but the sobs weren't within her power. "Lena, I love you. Please don't do this."

Chloe came out and held up her phone, completely unaware of what was taking place. "She's with Ben. He's bringing her home."

Lena started back up the walkway. "You're incapable of loving anything but yourself and your job. Go. Don't come back."

CHAPTER TWENTY

L ena sat in the living room with Laura and Chloe, watching as the man who had taken her parents, who had changed their lives forever, was walked into the police station on the six o'clock news.

"You should call her."

Lena looked at the two people closest to her in the world. "I'm not calling her."

"Lena, I asked her not to tell you. I begged her. She saw I was okay and that I was with Ben. Like I told you, I had a few drinks, but Ben was completely sober. If Amy thought I was in danger, she would have told you."

Lena continued to watch the television. She was angry, bitter, and devastated. "It doesn't matter what you asked her, she should have told me. Especially when I didn't know where you were. She should have told me right away."

"She called there to look for me though, even if it meant getting her client in trouble."

Lena huffed. "You wouldn't understand."

"You think that, but I do understand. I understand you were happier with Amy than I've ever seen you. I understand she made a mistake, and has been trying to make up for it, but you won't let her. And I understand people make mistakes and deserve second chances. I understand that last part because you've told me that my whole life. I don't understand why that applies to everyone but Amy." Laura kissed her on the cheek. "I'm going to bed. Please think about it."

After Laura had disappeared up the steps, Chloe finally spoke. "The kid has a point."

"She doesn't know anything. She's sixteen."

Chloe got off the other sofa and sat next to Lena. She held out her wrist that boasted the bracelet their mothers had shared. "Remember when we were sixteen?"

Lena looked down at her own matching bracelet. "You need to be more specific."

Chloe took her hand. "Remember when I told my mom I was staying at your house, when really I went to spend the night with Raymond?"

"I don't know what you ever saw in that guy."

"Let's stay on topic, shall we." She tapped Lena's leg. "Remember how he talked me into breaking into that backyard with him to go swimming and we got caught? I never thought my mom would forgive me, but you told me that as long as my apology was genuine and I never did something like that again, my mom would forgive me and eventually learn to trust me."

"It's not the same thing."

"You're right, it's not. Amy did the right thing, even if it wasn't as quickly as you would have liked."

"Laura could have really been hurt."

"She did the right thing even if it meant her client getting in trouble. She put her job at risk."

"She should have told me."

"Yes, she should have. But people aren't perfect, and she'll probably make a thousand more mistakes. But, honey, if you're waiting for a perfect person who never makes any mistakes, you may as well buy a one-way ticket on the single train for the rest of your life." She kissed Lena's cheek. "Just make sure you get a ticket right next to me. We can get cats, maybe a dog. I haven't worked out all the details yet."

Lean smiled. "What's wrong with it just being us?"

Chloe rubbed her hand. "Nothing. But you found something better AND you still get to keep me. Pretty cool, if you ask me."

Lena watched the images flash across the television, but she couldn't hear the words. Lena knew people weren't perfect. She understood there would be times that she would be let down. But Amy had crossed a line with Laura. She shuddered as all of the worst-case scenarios played through her head. Would it be possible to forgive Amy? The betrayal ran deep. Yes, Amy had eventually done the right thing, but at what cost? She knew how strongly she felt about Peter Reynolds and her sister being anywhere near him. Laura wasn't a passing phase or a pet. She was her little sister and her responsibility. Amy had proven she wasn't ready to be in a parenting role of any kind when she'd allowed her drunk little sister to leave the party and never have to deal with the consequences of her irresponsible behavior.

Kicking that idea around in her head for a few moments led her to all the mistakes she had made when she was suddenly saddled with the responsibility of caring for Laura. Was she being fair? Lena closed her eyes, wondering when life had become so complicated. *Amy, that's when it got complicated. Complicated, and pretty wonderful.* Maybe it was time to move forward.

Amy stretched the kinks in her back and grinned at her tablemates. Sarah adjusted the pink, glittery "Bride to Be" sash she wore across her body. Evelyn leaned back and handed her empty glass to a passing tray Amy assumed was attached to an actual human server, in the poorly lit bar. She never imagined she would be sitting at a table, in a bar, with Evelyn. They had run into each other at a work function and had managed to clear the air properly. It was awkward at first, but after a few lunches and several text messages, they had fallen into a comfortable friendship. It was nice being able to make amends with someone she felt had wronged her, someone whose actions she'd allowed to color her own for far too long. Amy had secretly hoped a small amount of forgiveness karma would come back to her in the form of Lena, but now she had actually grown to enjoy Evelyn's company.

Sarah leaned forward and burped. She covered her mouth, apparently surprised by the air escaping her body. "You should keep trying."

Amy patted her hand. "I called her every day for three weeks and she never answered. I'm actually surprised she didn't change her phone number."

Sarah raised her hands to stop her. Her words were slurred, something Amy would find annoying, normally, but it was actually pretty adorable on Sarah. "You can't give up on love, Amy!"

Amy took the drinks off the tray a server brought over and handed them out. She lifted hers toward Sarah and Evelyn. "It gave up on me."

Sarah took a sip. "Boo!"

Evelyn pointed across the room. "I hate to break up this uplifting conversation, but who is that brunette walking toward our table?"

Sarah patted Evelyn's arm. "That's Brittany. Her and Amy used to be a thing." The hiccup at the end of her sentence was a nice touch.

"I see. Is there anyone in San Francisco you haven't slept with?"

Sarah raised her hand. "Me!"

Brittany made it over to the table and sat next to Amy, swinging the chair around and sliding it between her legs. She put her hand out toward Evelyn. "Hi. I'm Brittany."

Evelyn took it and smiled her ridiculously seductive smile. "I've heard. I'm Evelyn."

Brittany smiled. "Nice to meet you."

Sarah interrupted. "Oh, Amy!" She smacked the table. "You need to know, Lena RSVP'd for the wedding."

Amy stared into her glass. "Perfect."

"With a plus one! Who do you think she's taking? Ohhhh…I bet she's pretty. She wouldn't date ugly women, I don't think."

Evelyn leaned over. "You should probably stop talking about that now."

Suddenly, all she could imagine was the variety of women Lena could choose to be with. "Who wants to do a round of shots?" *That should help.*

The possibility of Lena being with another woman made Amy's stomach hurt. Well, the images of Lena, along with the alcohol. She hadn't completely abandoned the thought of winning Lena back. She held on to it, an almost completely deflated life raft that she clung to for dear life. She felt the last bits of air drain out of her proverbial raft as she played back what Sarah had said about Lena bringing a plus one to the wedding.

She slammed a shot back, watching Evelyn and Brittany share flirtatious banter and touch each other's hands when a point in the conversation allowed. *So this is going to be a thing now.* She briefly pictured herself dramatically slamming her head against the table, but thought better of it. It was Sarah's night and it would be Sarah's day. She needed to put a brave face on and go to the wedding. She needed to brave the sight of Lena there with someone else and find a way to cope. That's all that there was left to do, cope.

Chapter Twenty-one

A my stood at the front of the small chapel. She looked out over the crowd of friends and family and was filled with a sense of happiness for her. She tried to ignore the bitter-sweetness of it, as she thought of Lena and the place she'd never have beside her. She glanced over at the fiercely nervous Matt. He was bouncing slightly on the balls of his feet as he stared down the empty aisle, waiting for Sarah and her father.

The "Bridal March" started playing, and everyone stood up as Sarah and her father entered the room. She looked beautiful, but that wasn't the best sight in the room. The best sight came from the groom, who wiped away a few tears as his bride moved slowly down the runner with her proud father.

Amy caught a glimpse of Lena in the back, but forced herself not to look. She wanted to be present in Sarah's moment, rather than dwelling on her own misstep. She watched as Matt placed a ring on Sarah's shaking hand. They exchanged the vows they had written themselves. Promises of forever, of support, of growing and mature love. The ceremony was perfect and quick, exactly what everyone likes. Amy's heart ached at the simple beauty of it, and she wondered if maybe, one day, she'd find something like that herself. She knew now she didn't want to spend the rest of her days having meaningless relationships with strangers. Lena had made her realize there was more to life than her job, and she was ready to find it. *Eventually*. She'd have to get over Lena first, and that was going to take a while.

Amy followed the rest of the bridal party out of the chapel, making sure not to make eye contact with Lena, though she could feel her fierce stare almost like a physical touch. It was the hardest thing she had ever done. She needed to put Lena out of her mind, and she definitely didn't want to see who she was with. The thought alone made her nauseous.

Amy had hoped the pictures would last longer. The reception was next, and she wasn't looking forward to having to inevitably face Lena. *Coward. Learn to face her, and maybe she'll at least respect you, even if she doesn't want you.* She tried to still her trembling hands and smiled politely at the guests around them.

❖

"Amy looks gorgeous."

Lena shot a look at Chloe.

"What? She does."

"I noticed."

Chloe popped another fried ravioli in her mouth. "I noticed that you noticed."

"Are you this articulate in court?"

Chloe pushed her. "I'm going to go cruise for single men." She made a shooing motion at Lena. "You should cruise for bridesmaids."

Lena rolled her eyes. "Nice try."

The truth was, she couldn't take her eyes off Amy. Usually bridesmaid's dresses weren't flattering, but today confirmed Amy was beautiful in everything she wore. Lena tried not to stare, but she couldn't manage to turn away. It had been a month since they had seen each other. The draw was still there. The unspoken connection they'd always shared was just as strong as it had always been. The realization was alarming and exhilarating.

Lena had actually been looking forward to the wedding. She wanted the opportunity to talk to Amy. She had decided a phone call wouldn't suffice at this point, and she had wanted to be able to look at Amy's eyes. To see her facial expression as they discussed what had put them here, and hopefully put it behind them. She hadn't planned on having that conversation at the wedding, but she wanted to know if Amy was open to it. She wanted to give it another try. She wanted Amy in her life, and all she could do was hope it wasn't too late. That they could somehow get past this.

Lena almost broke the glass she held in her hand when she saw her. Amy walked over to Evelyn, took her hand, and led her over to the table they were apparently sharing. Evelyn looked flawless in her red dress, red high heels, and perfectly red lipstick.

Chloe suddenly appeared by her side again and put an arm around her waist. "You know?" She nudged Lena's side. "That kind of perfection is boring anyway."

"Did you know she was coming?"

Chloe took a deep breath. "I did, but I didn't realize she was coming with Amy."

Lena finished her drink and set it on the table. She stood up and smoothed out the arms of her button-down silk shirt. As always, she felt inadequate next to Amy's ex. Lena felt a punch of jealousy hit her stomach, followed by the slow creeping of betrayal up her throat. Seeing Amy with Evelyn confirmed what she had been afraid of the first time she saw them together. *The draw of the first love will always be there.* Lena was worried she wouldn't measure up, and apparently, she didn't. "It's just as well, I guess. At least I didn't make a fool of myself. Can we get out of here?"

Chloe nodded. "Let's go say thank you to Matt and Sarah and go home."

Lena walked with Chloe through the tables covered with linen tablecloths, a variety of place settings, and three-foot-tall centerpieces. There were dozens of people laughing, talking, enjoying themselves, but Lena couldn't get out of there fast enough. When they finally reached the corner where Sarah and Matt were shaking hands and hugging excited friends and family, Lena felt a bit more relieved. She was out of Amy's line of site, and she would be able to make a fast escape.

Sarah grabbed her hands. "Lena! I'm so glad you made it, and I'm so glad you brought Chloe."

Chloe smiled, enjoying the compliment that seemed genuine.

Lena kissed her cheek and then hugged Matt. "It was a beautiful ceremony and the reception is fantastic. Thank you for inviting me."

"Have you seen Amy?" Sarah asked.

Matt put his hand on Sarah's back and winced, probably in an effort to remind her that Lena might not want to see Amy.

"I saw her, but I didn't talk to her. She was with someone."

Sarah looked disappointed. "Oh, okay."

Matt took Lena by the arm. "Can I talk to you for a minute?"

Lena followed him a few feet away from the others. "What's up, Matt?"

"I just wanted to see how you were doing? I saw the follow-up article Brittany wrote after the arrest, and it said you and Laura weren't available for comment."

Lena forced herself not to fidget. The truth was, between the finalization of the arrest, finding out she had an uncle, and the breakup with Amy, she wasn't feeling much like talking to anyone. Some days it was hard for her to even get out of bed. Reporters were always around the restaurant, and the interest generated by the article meant they were booked up seven nights a week. "Yeah, we're fine. I'm sorry I never returned any of your calls. There's just been a lot going on."

Matt nodded his understanding. "Can we get together for lunch when I get back from the honeymoon?"

Lena smiled at him and covered his hand with hers. He was a very sweet man, and his care and concern were genuine. "Yes, I would like that. I promise I'll answer this time."

He hugged her and kissed her cheek. "Thanks for coming. And you know, it's none of my business, but maybe you should return someone else's calls, too."

Lena waved for Chloe, who seemed to be in a very deep conversation with Sarah. A few moments later, they escaped out the back door.

Evelyn pointed to Lena and Chloe disappearing out the door. "She's leaving."

"What?" Amy looked around and saw Lena disappear around a corner. "Oh."

"You should go after her."

"What's the point? If she wanted to see me, she would have come over and talked to me. She's clearly trying to put me behind her."

"You're different now. She changed you."

Amy shrugged. "She just made me want to be better."

Evelyn leaned forward. "And you are. You quit your job and you're about to start work for one of the largest charities in the country. You haven't been with anyone since her; I've personally watched you blow off at least three different women. You aren't over her, and you should stop wasting time and go get what you want. Because there's one thing that hasn't changed—you are the most determined, driven person I know. Hearing 'no' has never stopped you before, and it shouldn't now."

"She was here with a date. I don't want to ruin anything."

Evelyn had a funny look on her face. "That wasn't a date... that was Chloe."

"What?"

"You know, Chloe. Tall, blond hair, sarcastic, great legs."

"I know who she is, smartass."

"Then why are you still sitting here talking to me?"

Amy leaned back in her chair, and rubbed her face. She thought briefly about going after her but changed her mind. Lena had made it pretty clear she wanted nothing to do with her, and she couldn't hear that kind of rejection come out of her mouth again. Amy knew she couldn't handle losing Lena all over again. *But she wasn't with a date. That's something.* She sighed and wished she could go home and cry.

CHAPTER TWENTY-TWO

M s. Kline, there's someone here to see you."
Amy pushed the button on her speakerphone.
"Sarah, come in here, please."

A few moments later, Sarah came through the doorway.
She was tan, relaxed, and Amy had never seen her happier.
Marriage looked good on her. When Amy had taken this job,
one of the stipulations she included in her hiring package was
that Sarah would be coming with her. It was in equal parts good
for her sanity and livelihood. "You go away for a few weeks on
a honeymoon, and suddenly we're back to you calling me Ms.
Kline at work?"

Sarah sat on the corner of Amy's desk, where she always
perched herself. "I don't know what the etiquette is here. We're
still new, and I want to make a good impression."

"We work for the Breast Cancer Foundation of America,
not the military. Call me Amy at work."

"Okay, boss." She winked at the end. "Oh, there really is
someone here to see you."

"Someone? Do they have a name?"

"I'll send her in." She started to walk out the door.

"Sarah, who is it?"

"They'll be right up."

A few minutes later, Chloe walked through her office door. Amy was surprised and happy to see her. She got up and walked around her desk. "Chloe, hi." She hugged her.

"I don't have a lot of time, so I'm going to make this quick."

Amy leaned against the front of her desk, and Chloe took a seat in the chair in front of her. "What's going on?"

"Lena is moving, and you need to go stop her. Tell her how you feel, how you messed up, blah, blah, blah. Fix this so we can keep her in town."

Amy felt slightly dizzy. *Lena's moving?* That didn't make sense, though. Lena would never give up her family's restaurant. "What about Lands End?"

"She gave up the full-time management to one of the managers. She and Laura are moving to San Diego. They said they needed to get away from this city and start over."

Amy didn't know what to say, but more than that, she was concerned about actually keeping her body upright. Being without Lena had been one of the most difficult things she had ever gone through, but knowing she was here in San Francisco made it bearable. Amy was able to hang on to some small amount of hope they would run into each other and things would work out, like in one of those romantic comedies Lena loved to watch. "When are they leaving?"

"She's packing a truck right now."

"You couldn't come to me earlier?" Amy grabbed her keys and her purse and headed out the door. She didn't bother to tell Sarah where she was going. She was sure Chloe would fill her in.

She drove through the busy streets of San Francisco, where people treated pedestrians as obstacles, like they were trapped inside a game of Mario Kart. Muni drivers whipped through the streets without a care in the world, and cabs pulled out in front of her as if they got extra money to do so. She was in front of Lena's house eleven minutes later. There was a truck parked out front. Lena was putting a desk in it, checking the knots that were tying it down in place. Amy got out of her car and ran across the street, which was an impressive feat in the six-inch heels she was wearing.

"You can't go."

Lena stood up in the back of the truck. "Amy?"

"You can't go."

Lena continued to stare at her blankly.

"I'm sorry. I messed up. I should have told you about Laura, but I didn't know what the right thing to do was. I wanted her to trust me, and I didn't think it was anything you had to know, because she was with Ben, and I really did believe she was okay. I made the mistake of not telling you. I know I messed up, I know I messed up bad, but I want another chance. We deserve another chance."

Lena hopped out of the truck and stood in front of her. The proximity threw Amy. She hadn't been this close to Lena in a little over a month, and she wanted to touch her. Instead, she continued to ramble. "I quit my job. I wasn't a very good person, and it's not just the job's fault, but it made me cross some lines I should have never crossed."

Lena kept staring at her.

"I can't stop thinking about you. I can't seem to get over you. I don't want to not be a part of your life anymore. Just tell me what I need to do to make you stay."

Lena looked confused. "Stay?"

Amy took a small step closer, needing to be within arm's reach. "Yes. Chloe came to my office and told me you and Laura were moving to San Diego because you needed to get out of San Francisco. I'm not saying you should stay just because of me, but if you leave, we'll never have a chance again, and you can't do that. Plus, you can't leave Lands End. I know it's not what you wanted, but it's part of you and—"

"Amy." Lena put her hands on her shoulders. "We aren't going anywhere. I'm donating some items to the halfway house my uncle is staying at."

Amy looked at the truck in the driveway. "You aren't moving?"

Lena laughed. "No. You just got played by Chloe."

Amy looked at the truck again. "I think I got played by Sarah and Chloe both."

Amy waited for Lena to say something else. Anything that would indicate she wanted to keep talking to her, that what she had told her mattered, that *she* mattered, but Lena just stood there. Amy backed away; it hurt as much as the last time she had walked down this driveway. The San Francisco summer sun that never seemed to run hot, suddenly felt excruciating on her warming skin. "Okay, well, I guess I'll see you around."

"Amy, wait."

Amy turned around. Lena was fidgeting with her hands. She looked like she wanted to say something else. Amy would stay stuck in this very spot for the next several months if it meant Lena was possibly going to speak to her.

"Did you really change jobs?"

"Yeah, I did."

"For me?"

Amy shook her head. "No, for me. But I realized I needed to make the change because of you."

Lena took a step closer. "Did you really mean what you said about not being over me?"

Amy took a step closer to her. "I did. I loved you then, and I love you now. That hasn't changed."

"What about Evelyn?" She took another step toward Amy.

"We're friends. That's all we've been, and all we'll ever be. I want you. Just you."

Lena looked at the sky. She seemed to be thinking about something. Amy wished she could read minds.

"It's hot. Do you want to come inside and get something to drink?" She put out her hand and Amy took it.

"Yes, I would really like that." The feel of Lena's hand, the relief that flooded her entire being, nearly made her drop to her knees and weep. Instead, she followed Lena into the house, praying to anyone listening that this meant what she hoped it did.

Lena sat at the island, and Amy could feel her eyes on her. That familiar stare she had grown to love and missed. It was intent, devoted. Amy had never felt a stare of devotion until Lena, and she never wanted it to stop. Amy took another sip of her water as Lena began to talk.

"When I went to Sarah and Matt's wedding, I wanted to talk to you, to work things out."

Amy put the glass down and came around the island. She put her hands on top of Lena's. "You did?"

Lena nodded. "Then I saw you with Evelyn, and I almost lost it. I thought you two had gotten back together."

Amy let out a laugh which was more like a long breath. "No, not even a little bit."

Lena took Amy's arms and placed them around her neck. "I wish I had known at the time."

"You should have asked."

"I should have. I should have done a lot of things. I should have answered your phone calls. I should have gone to your apartment. I should have told you I had forgiven you."

The relief that washed through Amy's body wasn't like anything she had ever felt before. "You forgive me?"

"Yes, Amy. I forgive you. I made so many mistakes when I first became Laura's guardian. There aren't enough walls in this house to write them all on. But you made a single mistake, and I instantly turned into a hypocrite. I'm sorry, too."

Amy hugged her. Partly because she wanted, needed, to be near her, and partly because she wanted to hold on to this moment for as long as she could. "Can we please try this again? Start over?"

Lena shook her head. "I don't want to start over. I want to pick up where we left off. The one thing that this month away from you has made painfully clear, is that I am in love with you. I want to be with you. I don't function very well without you, and I don't want to feel like that ever again."

Amy pulled back, so she could look into Lena's eyes. The warmth, the care, the love. It was all there, written almost like words in her ice blue eyes. "I love you too, and I'm not going anywhere."

EPILOGUE—DECEMBER OF THAT YEAR

L aura, get down here. We need to get to Lands End."
Footsteps rapidly descended the staircase. "I was on my way down. You don't need to yell."

"I wouldn't yell if you were capable of being anything that even slightly resembled being on time once in a while.

"Ugh! You're so bossy."

"Yes, I'm horrible."

They walked out to the car and drove the few miles to their family's restaurant. The weather had turned cold again, the fog was thick, and the streets were covered in holiday lights. It was reassuring that the seasons always changed, and even more comforting that they could be counted on to return once again.

"Oh good! Ben is already here!" Laura's face lit up when she saw the late nineties Honda Civic parked in the lot adjacent to the restaurant. "I haven't seen him in weeks."

Lena got out of the car and headed for the large double doors. "You aren't spending the night over there, so don't even ask."

Laura followed closely behind. "I wasn't going to. I know the rules."

Lena pulled the door open. "Yes, but knowing them and following them have never really lined up for you."

"You're so funny."

Lena's heart filled with love when she walked inside. Chloe was busy bossing people around, directing them where to set up tables and where to place donations. Ben was scribbling something on a clipboard.

Uncle Nathan was talking to a group of volunteers, explaining what their job would be for the next few hours. It had taken some time, but they had been able to start rebuilding bridges Lena had originally thought were burned forever. He really had stayed sober, and now worked as a server at Lands End. Lena had made him cut his beard and had bought him all new clothes, helped him find a shelter, and eventually his own place. They were taking it day by day, but things were moving in the right direction. She watched as Laura walked over and hugged him. It had actually been Laura who convinced her to give him another chance. She pointed out that all the charity work they did wouldn't mean anything if they couldn't find a way to help their own homeless uncle. Lena was proud of her. Laura was turning into an amazing young woman, and their parents would have been unbelievably proud.

"Sarah and Matt will be down in a bit. As always, they're running a bit late."

Lena smiled. She loved that voice; the calmness it exuded, along with love, passion, and appreciation. Amy appeared under her arm a moment later, draping Lena over her, and holding on to her hand. "Everything looks great. Thank you for helping."

Amy looked up at her and smiled. "I still think it's redundant that you're going to college for business management, but I'm proud of you for working so hard."

"Finishing school is really important to me."

"I know it is, and you're doing great. I'm happy to help whenever I can. You know I'm behind you, all the way." Amy patted her back. "The line is getting pretty long outside. You ready?"

Lena kissed the top of her head. So much had changed in the course of a year. Laura seemed to be on track, at least for now. Lena never knew what would happen week to week. Amy was engrained into their everyday lives, and she had never been happier. The loneliness that had once been a constant was now a distant memory. She wasn't sure what her future held, or where it would take her, but she did know one thing for sure—Amy would be there every step along the way. "Yes. Why don't you do the honors this time?"

Amy smiled up at her. Her eyes were filled with love, affection, and adoration. She walked over and pulled open the double doors. "Welcome to Lands End."

About the Author

Jackie D was born and raised in the San Francisco, East Bay area of California. She now resides in Central Pennsylvania with her partner and their numerous furry companions. She earned a bachelor's degree in recreation administration and a dual master's degree in management and public administration. She is a Navy veteran and served in Operation Iraqi Freedom as a flight deck director, onboard the USS *Abraham Lincoln*.

She spends her free time with her partner, friends, family, and their incredibly needy dogs. She enjoys playing golf but is resigned to the fact she would equally enjoy any sport where drinking beer is encouraged during game play. Her first book, *Infiltration,* was a finalist for a Lambda Literary Award.

Books Available from Bold Strokes Books

Basic Training of the Heart by Jaycie Morrison. In 1944, socialite Elizabeth Carlton joins the Women's Army Corps to escape family expectations and love's disappointments. Can Sergeant Gale Rains get her through Basic Training with their hearts intact? (978-1-62639-818-4)

Before by KE Payne. When Tally falls in love with her band's new recruit, she has a tough decision to make. What does she want more—Alex or the band? (978-1-62639-677-7)

Believing in Blue by Maggie Morton. Growing up gay in a small town has been hard, but it can't compare to the next challenge Wren—with her new, sky-blue wings—faces: saving two entire worlds. (978-1-62639-691-3)

Coils by Barbara Ann Wright. A modern young woman follows her aunt into the Greek Underworld and makes a pact with Medusa to win her freedom by killing a hero of legend. (978-1-62639-598-5)

Courting the Countess by Jenny Frame. When relationship-phobic Lady Henrietta Knight starts to care about housekeeper Annie Brannigan and her daughter, can she overcome her fears and promise Annie the forever that she demands? (978-1-62639-785-9)

Dapper by Jenny Frame. Amelia Honey meets the mysterious Byron De Brek and is faced with her darkest fantasies, but will her strict moral upbringing stop her from exploring what she truly wants? (978-1-62639-898-6E)

Delayed Gratification: The Honeymoon by Meghan O'Brien. A dream European honeymoon turns into a winter storm nightmare involving a delayed flight, a ditched rental car, and eventually, a surprisingly happy ending. (978-1-62639-766-8E)

For Money or Love by Heather Blackmore. Jessica Spaulding must choose between ignoring the truth to keep everything she has, and doing the right thing only to lose it all—including the woman she loves. (978-1-62639-756-9)

Hooked by Jaime Maddox. With the help of sexy Detective Mac Calabrese, Dr. Jessica Benson is working hard to overcome her past, but they may not be enough to stop a murderer. (978-1-62639-689-0)

Lands End by Jackie D. Public relations superstar Amy Kline is dealing with a media nightmare, and the last thing she expects is for restaurateur Lena Michaels to change everything, but she will. (978-1-62639-739-2)

Lysistrata Cove by Dena Hankins. Jack and Eve navigate the maelstrom of their darkest desires and find love by transgressing gender, dominance, submission, and the law on the crystal blue Caribbean Sea. (978-1-62639-821-4)

Twisted Screams by Sheri Lewis Wohl. Reluctant psychic Lorna Dutton doesn't want to forgive, but if she doesn't do just that an innocent woman will die. (978-1-62639-647-0)

A Class Act by Tammy Hayes. Buttoned-up college professor Dr. Margaret Parks doesn't know what she's getting herself into when she agrees to one date with her student, Rory Morgan, who is 15 years her junior. (978-1-62639-701-9)

Bitter Root by Laydin Michaels. Small town chef Adi Bergeron is hiding something, and Griffith McNaulty is going to find out what it is even if it gets her killed. (978-1-62639-656-2)

Capturing Forever by Erin Dutton. When family pulls Jacqueline and Casey back together, will the lessons learned in eight years apart be enough to mend the mistakes of the past? (978-1-62639-631-9)

Deception by VK Powell. DEA Agent Colby Vincent and Attorney Adena Weber are embroiled in a drug investigation involving homeless veterans and an attraction that could destroy them both. (978-1-62639-596-1)

Dyre: A Knight of Spirit and Shadows by Rachel E. Bailey. With the abduction of her queen, werewolf-bodyguard Des must follow the kidnappers' trail to Europe, where her queen—and a battle unlike any Des has ever waged—awaits her. (978-1-62639-664-7)

First Position by Melissa Brayden. Love and rivalry take center stage for Anastasia Mikhelson and Natalie Frederico in one of the most prestigious ballet companies in the nation. (978-1-62639-602-9)

Best Laid Plans by Jan Gayle. Nicky and Lauren are meant for each other, but Nicky's haunting past and Lauren's societal fears threaten to derail all possibilities of a relationship. (987-1-62639-658-6)

Exchange by CF Frizzell. When Shay Maguire rode into rural Montana, she never expected to meet the woman of her dreams—or to learn Mel Baker was held hostage by legal agreement to her right-wing father. (987-1-62639-679-1)

Just Enough Light by AJ Quinn. Will a serial killer's return to Colorado destroy Kellen Ryan and Dana Kingston's chance at love, or can the search-and-rescue team save themselves? (987-1-62639-685-2)

Rise of the Rain Queen by Fiona Zedde. Nyandoro is nobody's princess. She fights, curses, fornicates, and gets into as much trouble as her brothers. But the path to a throne is not always the one we expect. (987-1-62639-592-3)

Tales from Sea Glass Inn by Karis Walsh. Over the course of a year at Cannon Beach, tourists and locals alike find solace and passion at the Sea Glass Inn. (987-1-62639-643-2)

The Color of Love by Radclyffe. Black sheep Derian Winfield needs to convince literary agent Emily May to marry her to save the Winfield Agency and solve Emily's green card problem, but Derian didn't count on falling in love. (987-1-62639-716-3)

A Reluctant Enterprise by Gun Brooke. When two women grow up learning nothing but distrust, unworthiness, and abandonment, it's no wonder they are apprehensive and fearful when an overwhelming love just won't be denied. (978-1-62639-500-8)

Above the Law by Carsen Taite. Love is the last thing on Agent Dale Nelson's mind, but reporter Lindsey Ryan's investigation could change the way she sees everything—her career, her past, and her future. (978-1-62639-558-9)

Actual Stop by Kara A. McLeod. When Special Agent Ryan O'Connor's present collides abruptly with her past, shots are fired, and the course of her life is irrevocably altered. (978-1-62639-675-3)

Embracing the Dawn by Jeannie Levig. When ex-con Jinx Tanner and business executive E. J. Bastien awaken after a one-night stand to find their lives inextricably entangled, love has its work cut out for it. (978-1-62639-576-3)

Jane's World: The Case of the Mail Order Bride by Paige Braddock. Jane's PayBuddy account gets hacked and she inadvertently purchases a mail order bride from the Eastern Bloc. (978-1-62639-494-0)

Love's Redemption by Donna K. Ford. For ex-convict Rhea Daniels and ex-priest Morgan Scott, redemption lies in the thin line between right and wrong. (978-1-62639-673-9)

The Shewstone by Jane Fletcher. The prophetic Shewstone is in Eawynn's care, but unfortunately for her, Matt is coming to steal it. (978-1-62639-554-1)

A Touch of Temptation by Julie Blair. Recent law school graduate Kate Dawson's ordained path to the perfect life gets thrown off course when handsome butch top Chris Brent initiates her to sexual pleasure. (978-1-62639-488-9)

Beneath the Waves by Ali Vali. Kai Merlin and Vivien Palmer love the water and the secrets trapped in the depths, but if Kai gives in to her feelings, it might come at a cost to her entire realm. (978-1-62639-609-8)

Girls on Campus edited by Sandy Lowe and Stacia Seaman. College: four years when rules are made to be broken. This collection is required reading for anyone looking to earn an A in sex ed. (978-1-62639-733-0)

Heart of the Pack by Jenny Frame. Human Selena Miller falls for the domineering Caden Wolfgang, but will their love survive Selena learning the Wolfgangs are werewolves? (978-1-62639-566-4)

Miss Match by Fiona Riley. Matchmaker Samantha Monteiro makes the impossible possible for everyone but herself. Is mysterious dancer Lucinda Moss her own perfect match? (978-1-62639-574-9)

Paladins of the Storm Lord by Barbara Ann Wright. Lieutenant Cordelia Ross must choose between duty and honor when a man with godlike powers forces her soldiers to provoke an alien threat. (978-1-62639-604-3)

Lightning Source UK Ltd.
Milton Keynes UK
UKOW02f0656170916

283208UK00001B/16/P